toxic ii

GENERATIONAL CURSES

PENNY BLACWRITE

contents

penny blacwrite catalog

mailing list

Thank you so much for your continuous support, Residents of Pennyville. You've been rocking with me for twelve books. I am so appreciative. Make sure you are SUBSCRIBED to my mailing list. Click here to subscribe.

penny's reader community

Thank you so much for your continued support! Use the QR code to follow me on social media.

playlist

"Casamigos"- Sukihana ft. Afro B
"Young Rich Niggas"- Migos
"Rehab"- Amy Winehouse
"Superwoman" - Chrisette Michele
"Gold Digger"- Kanye West
"Going Viral"- Fivio Foreign
"Lost One"- Jay Z ft. Chrisette Michele
"Lost Ones"- Lauryn Hill
"Sex Me"- R. Kelly
"In The Kitchen"- R. Kelly
"Make Her Feel Good"- Teyana Taylor
"Hrs & Hrs"- Muni Long

synopsis

Meet Darren "Dice" Bleeker, the don of all dons, star college basketball player, and BBW lover. He's at the top of his game. He has everything a young, rich man could want — millions void of blood money, or illegal activities — pure generational WEALTH. However, with generational wealth comes generational curses, mind-blowing secrets, forbidden romances, and even murder. You're in for a wild ride with Dice.

Read *Toxic: A Forbidden Romance* to get a rich history of Dice's backstory and an inside look into the traumas and generational curses he was born into despite his glamorous lifestyle now.

previously in toxic: a forbidden romance

the ultimate sacrifice

Bonita Bleeker

I hadn't heard from Imani since we were all at the estate office for the paternity tests. Considering that I didn't have to take one myself, I had no idea if the results had come back. All I knew was that I hadn't heard anything from Imani or Don, so I was in the clear. Well, slightly, but not really. I still had to face my baby boy Dennis and tell him about his father's death. Not only that, but I had to break it to both of the boys that their father requested to be cremated so there would be no funeral.

This is exactly why I had to head out two hours to Clayton, Georgia, to get Dennis from his day camp a few days earlier. They both, including Imani, deserved to see their father once more before the cremation process. Rob's body was stored in the funeral home he requested, while I still didn't get a chance to sign off on the cremation.

Since I had stalled a few days, there was still enough time to get Dennis so he could say goodbye, and I was determined to do right by Rob. It was the least I could do in respect of his wishes. So, after calling Imani and getting no response, Darren and I made our way out to Blue Ridge Summer Camp. While I would have loved Imani's company, I was relieved she was unavailable. I didn't want her blabbing her mouth to the boys. They didn't need to hear their father's nasty remarks about them, and I would do whatever necessary to make sure they never heard it.

As we rode through the mountainous terrain, admiring the skyline, Darren was pretty quiet. I could tell he wasn't pissed off because he continued to bop his head to the music and gawk at sights as we drove by. Although he stayed quiet, I didn't trip over it. Truthfully, I was at a loss for words as well and just wanted to enjoy the ride.

After an hour of driving and enjoying the music and each other's company, Darren turned to me. "Momma, how are we going to break the news to Dennis? I don't think he can handle it," he stated with a weak crack in his voice.

The sound of my baby losing his strength stung my heart. I looked over at him while rearing the car's steering wheel tighter.

"I know, baby, but he's got us. He's got me, and most importantly, he's got you, his big brother. You two have always been there for each other, and this time is no different. Be the older, protective brother you were born to be, and if you need strength to give to Dennis, know Momma will always be right here!" I consoled.

Darren exhaled out and sat back in his seat with a

slight grin. My baby was hurting, but at least he lightened my heart with that forced smile. It gave me the hope I needed to know my boys would be okay.

<hr>

My younger baby boy, Dennis, came running out of the lodge with his suitcase in tow and a toasted toffee complexion. The sun sure did a number on him, which became more apparent as he approached the car, confused.

"Don't look so disappointed to see us. We missed you!" I gushed as I stepped out of the car to help him with his bag. Dennis was never easy to fool, so as soon as he caught a glimpse of Darren sitting in the front seat, he huffed and jerked his head back.

"What are you doing here? Ain't you supposed to be at work?" Dennis gasped.

Darren shot him a chilling look and yawned. "Just get in the damn car!" he huffed.

As I watched my baby climb into the back seat, I took my time before getting into the car myself. My hands were jittering, and my heart was beating. This was one of the hardest things I had to do. So, as soon as we drove off, I made a grand suggestion. "Find me the nearest Dave & Buster's. We're going to have some fun before we head back home!" I exclaimed.

"I'm down! Sounds like a plan!" Dennis squealed, which I was happy to hear.

After not hearing a peep from Darren, I turned to him and saw he was cornered by the window, staring aimlessly ahead to where I caught a reflective glimpse of his dead expression. The next few hours were going to be a struggle indeed.

The entire way to Dave and Buster's, I kept the stereo bumping with all the latest NBA YoungBoy tunes just to entertain Dennis and Darren. Things were going fine, but my body still jumped involuntarily every ten minutes. I just couldn't hold this news any longer. It was killing me internally, so I pulled over to the next rest stop I spotted.

"You read my mind, Momma. I need some hot Cheetos and candy. You think they got any hot pickles at this one?" Dennis excitedly quizzed.

I ignored his question and pulled up near the dumpsters behind the entrance of the gas station. Darren was mute the entire time as I put the car in park. He didn't budge, not one bit.

For some reason, Dennis caught Darren's energy drift and became suspicious.

"Momma, what's going on? You came to get me early from camp and brought Darren, who hasn't been up here in years. He hates Blue Ridge. Then, during this entire ride, he's been quiet the whole time." Dennis badgered me with his accusations.

I took a deep breath and let a loud sigh come out. "Dennis, I have something to tell you."

"What, Momma?" he probed with an annoyed disposition.

"While you were away at camp—" I started to explain.

"Dad is gone. He's fucking dead, Dennis, and it's

nothing we can do about it!" Darren sneered, cutting me off as he looked over his seat toward his brother.

"Daddy's dead? How? When? What?" Dennis screamed, demanding answers as he stared at me.

"A little over a month ago, your father was admitted to the hospital for issues with his vision. After a few weeks of tests, he got out of the hospital bed and hit his head on the bed rail, and it punctured through his eye socket. Baby, I'm so sorry I didn't tell you sooner. I just didn't have the heart at the time to come all the way up here and face you," I sniveled.

Staring back at me with a puffy face and red eyes, Dennis sat in a stooped posture with a caved chest. I just crushed his little heart, and there was nothing that could be undone to erase the pain he'd experienced for years to come.

We drove all the way home in silence. The tension in the car was stifling, choking me despite how much free air and oxygen circulated. Although the air conditioning was pumping, it wasn't until I parked in front of the house and hopped out of the car that I was able to breathe. The humid moisture helped the air in my lungs return. I slammed the car door shut and hurried into the house while Darren and Dennis straddled behind me.

I rushed into my bedroom, slammed the door, and fell onto the bed. The pillow top mattress soothed my back, which was carrying the weight of the entire world. Never had my bed ever felt this damn good. But never had I needed comfort like this in life before. My world was crumbling in my face. I watched it play out this entire time, unveiling secrets I built an entire life off of.

Now, I had to walk around with this enormous amount of guilt that was piercing my soul all because I loved a man so much and could never leave him alone. The smoke and mirrors were gone, and it was clear for everyone to see. I just wanted to hide in my bed forever and escape it all, but I knew that would be short-lived, especially once I felt my phone vibrating at the end of the bed. I sighed as I sat up and reached for it.

A quick glance revealed Don's name, so I answered it. On the other side of the phone, I was met by heavy breathing and a muffled voice.

"You fucking bitch," he snarled. "All these years! All these fucking years, you never told me that Imani was mine. I asked you three times, and you lied, and each time, I believed you. How could you do this to me? How could you keep my daughter away from me?" he cried.

Emotion welled up in my heart, forcing tears to form in my eyes. Every bit of his words were eating me alive. I could hear Don wheezing, struggling for air as his cries got heavier.

"This is all your fault! I slept with my own daughter because you were never woman enough to tell the truth. You thought you could erase our sins by hiding them this long, just for everything to blow up in our faces... in my face! How could you be so selfish? You know I always wanted a little girl!" he heaved.

I didn't know what to say, so I stayed quiet. After a few seconds of silence, Don's pitch elevated. "Answer me!" he demanded.

However, I couldn't because he was right. I was wrong and selfish, costing myself the pursuit of happiness. I couldn't stop thinking that maybe we would have been together if I had told Don the truth all along. Perhaps I could have saved myself years of misery and heartache.

From the end of Don's line, I heard a mixture of rambling and heavy breathing.

"Oh my god, why didn't I demand a paternity test years ago when you popped up pregnant? I should have listened to myself. I should've never trusted you!" he screamed.

Hearing his heckle through the phone was heartbreaking. The wheezing in his chest became more pronounced before the line went dead. I hopped out of bed quickly because the call ending so abruptly put me on edge. Deep in my gut, I felt like I needed to rush to Don's house. He didn't sound too well, and I feared what he might do. So, while I wet my face and got myself together, all I thought about was the clock. A mental countdown went off in my head, producing a strong sense of urgency to hurry the fuck up and get to Don's house before something terrible happened.

I lied to the boys and told them I was heading to Walmart and Kroger to get some food. I had to add in both stores so they wouldn't get suspicious and worried. I rushed out of our gated community and made my way through the back skirts straight to I-20. I cut the radio off and rode in silence.

The closer I got to his exit, the faster my heartbeat and the stronger the flutters in my stomach got. I felt like I was drunk with butterflies and fear at the same time. Although I couldn't put my finger on it, I knew that whatever I was feeling wasn't good. This caused me to haul down the highway at ninety miles an hour, with no care in the world if I got stopped.

As I pulled up in front of Don's mansion, his car was sitting right in front of the circular driveway rather than in the garage where the rest of his vehicles were parked. I stepped out of my car, made my way to the entrance, and noticed that his door was cracked open. A feeling of doom came over me as soon as I entered the home, although it was meticulously clean and tidy.

"Don!" I shouted as I walked through the living room, admiring the beautiful paintings on the walls. They were by Leroy Campbell, a famous Black painter.

Campbell's paintings were rich and powerful as they featured Black people living life with no eyes or mouths. This distinction in his paintings made him a well-renowned artist and one of Don's favorites.

I smiled as I approached one of the paintings on the wall, admiring the hues and depth on the canvas. Flashbacks of Don and I visiting his art gallery in Brooklyn, New York, some years ago invaded my mind. Don and I had some wonderful memories. I let my finger trail along the features of the paintings before turning away to find Don.

After repeatedly calling out his name, he still hadn't responded, so I got really worried. I continued to walk around the first floor of the mansion, calling his name out and not getting a response until I made my way to the second floor in search of his room.

All along the walk, step by step, I called out his name. "Don!" I shouted. "Greedy, I see your car outside! Stop playing! I need to talk to you! Where are you?" I questioned as I finally made my way to the top of the stairs.

Standing across the hall was his room that I rushed into. At first glance, it was neat and spotless. There was no sign of Don or a burglar... at first, until I looked toward the master bathroom and saw a trail of blood leading out the door, staining the bedroom carpet.

I held my hands to my face, covering my mouth as I inched closer and closer to the bathroom, literally petrified by what I was about to see. Once in front of the slightly open door, I kicked it open and saw Don passed out on the floor in a pool of blood. Next to him was a Glock and a shell casing.

Hyperventilating, I let out an agonizing groan and dropped to the floor. Tears pained my face as I cuddled next to him on the floor while tugging at his dead weight. He wasn't breathing, and there was no pulse. I was at a loss for words. All I could communicate were wails and cries. This was all my fault. Don took his life because of me. The guilt continued to weigh me down as I rocked his body back and forth and kissed his lips.

"I'm so sorry. I'm so sorry," I mustered out, truly devastated.

Rob was gone, and now Don was gone. The feeling of being alone to raise my boys and even breaking the news to

Imani was paining me. I just didn't have the strength, so I continued to lie next to him, sobbing and sobbing, until I just couldn't resist the hopeless thoughts in my mind and reached over for the gun.

Shaking with the gun in my hand as I sat with my knees to my chest, I pulled the lever back and took a deep breath. I inserted the gun into my mouth, feeling every ridge of the hard steel. I forced the gun deeper into my mouth and gripped my lips tight around the steel.

I just couldn't take all the pain, the misery, the lying, the secrets, the abandonment, and the cheating anymore. It all just needed to stop, and I was determined to end it myself, and I did. I tapped the trigger, and the last thing I remembered was the crisp white and gray towelettes that hung on Don's shelf.

the last day

Imani Bleeker

Reading that there was a zero percent chance Don was my father was the best news I've heard in a long time. Although I knew there was no way I was his daughter because I always felt a strong connection to my dad, there were small moments of doubt. I was so nervous and anxious, just hoping that the results would denounce paternity. Being that the results did reveal Don wasn't my father, I was able to pick Crissy up from her job with the good news.

As I pulled up to Grady Hospital a little after five o'clock, I texted Crissy and told her I was downstairs. Five minutes later, she scurried out the front door wearing green scrubs and a hairnet covering her loose, curly, natural hair. Her face perked up when she saw me, and she ripped the net off her head and started twerking in the parking lot.

"A bitch is off and ready for a drink!" she shouted before getting in the car.

"Well, let's go, bitch!" I grinned.

Crissy let out a loud snort and put her seat belt on.

"Bitch, I got the results back!" I squealed.

Crissy turned to me and nervously smiled.

"And..." she speculated.

"And... he is *not* the father!" I joshed, imitating Maury Povich.

"Yessss, bitch! Yess, so you can still get your man back!" she exclaimed, which brought a solemn feeling to my heart. Crissy caught wind and rested her hand on my thigh. "Now come on, girl. You're supposed to be happy!"

"I know, but..." My words were cut off by vomit that unexpectedly came spilling out of my mouth.

Crissy instantly jumped out of the car, stripped out of her top, which revealed her bra, and began wiping the vomit off my mouth, leg, and the steering wheel.

As I wiped my mouth with my hand, Crissy put her index finger up, signaling me to wait. "I'll be right back. I'm going to get a spare outfit I have in my locker and something to clean this up," Crissy informed me.

I sat in throw-up while Crissy ran inside topless. After a few minutes of queasiness, I rested my head on the window, waiting for Crissy to return. When she did, she was completely cleaned up, and she had a bag full of sanitizer, gloves, a sheet, a change of clothes, a few rolls of paper towels, and a container of Lysol wipes. Crissy tended to me like the exceptional nurse she was while I sat quietly like a helpless patient.

Crissy was quiet at first, but once she got the car cleaned up, she looked at me seriously. "When's the last time you got your period?"

Thrown off guard, I cocked my head to the side and pondered. Hmm.

"Uhh, I didn't get it last month around the grand opening and figured it was late like usual during a high-stress time."

"Okay, and what about this month?" She questioned.

"It was supposed to be here last week," I gasped.

Crissy looked at me intently.

"Baby girl, you are pregnant. Do you want me to run inside and get you a few tests just so we can confirm it, although I'm sure that your ass is knocked up?"

I fumbled in my hair and squished my eyebrows together. "Pregnant? I can't be pregnant..." I sputtered, my words trailing off as I spoke.

"Well, there's only one way to be sure. Take a pregnancy test!" Crissy insisted.

"I will," I assured.

"Okay, okay. Give me a few minutes. I'll be right back," Crissy announced as she climbed out of the car.

"No, Crissy, it's fine. I'm going to get one from CVS and take it with Don. I'm so sorry, but I have to go. I'll send you one hundred dollars for an Uber and food," I expressed before hauling off, leaving Crissy standing there with a bewildered glare written on her face.

I jetted off in a quickness because I knew Crissy was right. I was pregnant. I just knew it. I just felt it in the pits of my stomach. Now, the entire way toward Don's place, after I stopped to pick up the test, I paid keen attention to the pressure I felt in my pelvis. It was a dull, persistent pressure that had been here for two weeks, but I had paid it no mind.

After all the drama these last two months, I didn't even stop to think about my menstrual. Once I moved in with Don and we officially took the condom off, I completely disregarded my period. Living with Don was the first time I didn't have to clock my menstrual cycle or track the days. I was finally with someone I trusted and could be completely free with.

At first, when Crissy mentioned the word pregnancy, I wasn't moved, but as I made my way to Don's, excitement and joy filled my heart. A baby was really growing inside of me. Don and I could finally be together, and bringing a new life to the world after my father died didn't sound so bad. Those thoughts forced me to push through traffic swiftly and get to Don's house.

As I pulled up to the house, I was surprised to see my momma's and Don's car parked out front. Anxious, I rolled my shoulders back and twisted my neck before approaching the door, unprepared for whatever I was about to witness. My knees began to buckle while an annoyingly persistent feeling stung my heart. *I couldn't fathom walking on them making love. That would kill me.*

I walked slowly up the stairs toward the bedroom. Once inside, my eyes leered directly to the bathroom, following a stream of blood. I tiptoed toward the bathroom and slid through the door, where my momma was sprawled out on top of Don as they both lay dead. I dropped my phone at the horrific sight, and instantaneously, my vision went black.

the hope of zion

Imani

I got up from the hot, uncomfortable seat, hoping to get some relief from how tightly the chairs were propped together. With my jumbo-sized umbrella open, I stood boldly, happy to stretch my legs, not giving a damn about blocking the view from the people behind me. It was a muggy, humid day, with a high of 102 degrees, and sitting in the open heat in the bleachers at Truist Park Stadium didn't make it any better.

Nonetheless, I was happy to be there and watch my baby brother Darren graduate from high school. Despite all he had been through between Daddy's and Momma's deaths in the last few years, he still managed to graduate on time and secure several college acceptances and scholarships. He fought hard with me to get better. We did the work. We went to counseling, we went to church, and we stayed prayed up. Although it hurt very much to be all alone in this world, so young with no parents, at least we had each other.

Snapping me out of my thoughts, Dennis tapped my leg, revealing a sweaty, red face. He threw his hands up, shoving my baby boy in my direction. "He wants his mother, Imani." Dennis huffed as he passed Zion to me, who was unusually fussy, kicking and swinging his feet in the air. I grabbed him, coddling his toddler body, and the dismay on his face instantly turned into a giggly coo. I kissed both of his cheeks, then tickled him with my nose, and he let out a loud laugh.

"Mommy's here, Zion. Mommy's here," I reassured him as I balanced all his twenty-seven pounds while holding the umbrella with my neck to properly place him on my hip.

Once situated, I held the umbrella in one hand as we watched Darren's class get called on one by one. Multi-tasking as usual, something I'd grown accustomed to since becoming a mother.

Zion, my eighteen-month-old son, laid his head on my collarbone, snuggling under the shade from the umbrella. His sweet, milky scent always soothed me, regardless of how tough the days were and how heavy they became. The weight of having someone rely on me day in and day out gave me a level of strength I didn't know I had. Most days, Zion was all I had to get through. His infectious smile would melt my heart whenever I had finished crying uncontrollably, thinking about Momma, Daddy, and Don all being gone.

As I rocked Zion back and forth, I strained my eyes onto the baseball field where the graduates were seated in several rows of white plastic chairs, looking for Darren... third row, eighth seat. He was seated up front since the graduating class was organized alphabetically, which meant his name should be called at any minute.

I fixed my stare back to the stage where the administration staff convened. The principal stood with the mic to his mouth as he called the next name. "Reginald Baker," he announced as the crowd erupted in cheer.

Full of anticipation, I playfully kicked Dennis. "Stand up. Darren is about to be called," I instructed Dennis.

Dennis, stocky and pudgy, hadn't taken the loss of Mom and Daddy too well. He'd been struggling the most, from overeating to depression and isolation. I was thankful enough that we were able to get him out of the house today. Dennis stood up perky, with a fixed grin on his face as he leaned forward, focused on the graduates sitting below on the baseball field.

"Excuse me, can you move over a bit?" a middle-aged white woman said, elbowing Dennis in the side as she stretched for room.

Uncomfortable, Dennis shot me an annoyed glare and moved closer to me. I glanced around, eyeing the attendees who were all dressed in their graduation best to watch their loved ones walk across the stage and receive their diplomas, just like me. Our tight section was cramped with no empty seats. We were literally on top of each other like roaches.

Zion was falling asleep, and I knew it because I felt the

heaviness of his small little head weighing me down. As I rocked back and forth, managing to stay leveled in my four-inch-tall platform sandals, the principal motioned to the middle of the stage.

"The next name I am going to call is a student who has made us all proud, securing full-ride scholarships at UCLA, Duke University, Howard University, and Seton Hall University. Despite the tragic and horrific challenges that have plagued him, he has continued to push on and make us proud. With that said, we would like to present the Overachiever's Award and a check for twenty-five hundred dollars to none other than Darren Bleeker!"

Excitement took over me, and I blustered into a loud cheer. "Let's go, Darren! Let's go, brotherrrrr!" I exaggerated as I wailed and clapped obnoxiously, not giving two fucks about waking Zion up or being gawked at.

Zion raised his head and started squirming in my arm, showing his slight discomfort as I watched Darren stroll onto the stage and grab his diploma and award. Baby bro was elated. His face lit up with a bright smile. He was glowing, and it felt so damn good to watch.

"You see Uncle Darren? He's a grown man now," I whispered to Zion as a tear fell from my eye. Proud was an understatement.

After nearly losing my voice, I sat down, still holding my umbrella, blocking out the sun from beaming on Zion and me. I looked down at my hands as I tapped my foot up and down, soothing my baby boy, who sat on my lap.

To think that in the matter of two years, I was a mother, a parental guardian to my two brothers, and a Black entrepreneur with three boutique locations throughout Atlanta was crazy to me. I went from a recent college graduate to a real woman quickly. Both Momma and Daddy's estates were left to me, totaling a whopping one hundred million dollars, allowing me to expand the boutique and create brokerage accounts for Darren and Dennis. I put thirty million each in their accounts and bought them both new cars. Seeing as Don also left me one-third of his estate with a dear letter to his "goddaughter", I didn't really need my parents' money. Don's estate was triple Momma and Daddy's, at six hundred and thirty-seven million dollars. Two-thirds of his estate was split between his three sons, Devin, Deon, and Donnell. They were all mad as fuck the day they called me to meet them at the estate planner's office two years ago. Their deadpan stares and grave mannerisms were so dry that it almost cut me in the heart when they refused to address me.

Nonetheless, I walked out of there with two hundred and twelve million dollars while all three of them split four hundred million dollars. They may have felt a little slighted, but truthfully, their bank accounts were sitting pretty nicely. Since they were so upset with me, I wondered how they would have felt to split their two-thirds by five instead of three, but we'd never know because I decided to keep my mouth shut.

There was no proof that Darren and Dennis were Don's biological sons, and I had no intention of making any waves. I was just happy that I could take care of my brothers, myself, and my son. Thankfully, with the amount of money I had in the bank and the income my boutique was bringing in, at one hundred thousand dollars a month after overhead, Zion, Darren, Dennis, and I were set for life.

Staying in our parents' house was too emotionally taxing, so we rented it out on Airbnb and Vrbo and moved into another house in Duluth. Being that we had lost our parents, it felt good living together. It felt like a real home. Zion had male figures to look up to. The boys had me, a female role model to nurture and love on them, and I had them all to keep me strong and moving. God was good, even in the midst of a bad storm. With all the trauma from the last two years, I was finally able to breathe, knowing that everything would be alright.

five years later...

trouble in paradise

Darren "Dice" Bleeker

"Fuck! I'm about to nut. Damn, that pussy just gets better and better," I praised Tati as she threw it back, clapping that fat juicy, supple ass all over my dick.

Her shit looked like a tsunami, waving and pulsing, and I was just making my way through it on a surfboard, not afraid to get drenched in that motherfucker if I had to.

"Yes, daddy. Keep going. Keep fucking me! Just like that," she begged, and so I continued strumming her wet, creamy cat, with her asshole staring back at me as she held the perfect position, arched over in our canopy-styled bed.

Considering that I was much taller than her, standing at six-foot-three, I had to lower my knees onto the bed frame to really get in them guts.

I loved my girlfriend Tati not just because she was a

BBW and had some of the tightest, wettest pussy I ever had but because she knew how to take my meaty, nine-inch dick while talking shit at the same time.

"Fuck me like a slut, daddy. Fuck me like your slut!" she hollered.

I smirked, happy that I was on the verge of busting. This was our third round, and I had to finish up so I could hit the gym for practice. As much as I loved Tati, I couldn't let her drain all my energy.

"Ouu, I'm about to cum, daddy," her shaky voice echoed the magic words. I loved it when we came together.

"You've been keeping up with the pill, right?" I managed to ask, my head spinning as I was fixated on the massive waves coming from her gigantic ass.

"Nah, babe. Nut on my face and record it for my Only Fans," she purred, her falsetto intoxicated with lust.

Disappointed, that's when I slid right out of her pussy. Although I didn't want to, she turned me all the way off. Some things were just personal and not for the world to see.

"I told you I was only okay with you sucking my dick on camera because of the ski mask you be wearing. Why in the fuck would I want my girl to be showing her face for the world to see with a dick in her mouth?" I exhaled deeply as rage seeped into my veins, and anger filtered through my breath.

Tati's cheeks were flushed with embarrassment and a perky blush of humiliation as she stood stunned like a hoe in headlights. "But it's your dick, baby! Imagine how much money we could make if they got to see you nutting on my pretty face?" She grinned, her sexy smile and quirky lisp now irritating the shit out of me.

I was so tired of hearing Tatiana talk about money. It was draining.

"You talk about money with me every day as if you don't know who you're fucking. Does it look like I need money? Does it look like I need heat from the athletic department, my boys, and others behind you sucking my dick online?" My voice pierced through the room, causing my dick to go numb. She had fucked up my mood just when I was about to cum talking that bullshit.

"Look, Darren, I know you're set for life. I know your parents left you a lot of money, and I know your sister is one of Atlanta's biggest entrepreneurs, but that's your reality, not mine," she argued as she got up from the bed in her birthday suit.

Tati's chestnut-complected triple D cups were swinging as her hardened nipples pointed to her feet. The dimples in her cheeks deepened as she flashed me a surprisingly coy simper, not to mention her soft, pillowing fupa cupped over the hump of her camel's toe, looking so soft, I wanted to lay my head on it.

Man, that pussy was so good. Why she had to fuck up my nut?

"But you're my girl. Whatever is mine is yours. How many times do I have to keep explaining that to you? I'm already paying your car note and cell phone bill and covering all our monthly expenses in this expensive ass condo. I give you an allowance, and I still pay for your hair and nails, and you get to go shopping whenever you feel like it. What fucking more do you want from me?" Tati had any and everything she asked for.

"That's the thing. I don't want anything from you. I want to be self-sufficient. I want to provide for myself, Darren. We aren't married. What you do for me isn't enough because, at any point in time, it can all just stop, and I'd still have to take care of myself," Tati complained, her whiny pitch gnawing at me.

The one thing I hated about Tati was how worrisome she was. She would work herself up in a panic, obsessing over the future, when she had support from everywhere — me, financial aid, and not to mention her parents were still alive. I, on the other hand, had to feign for myself. While both of my parents may have left me a large inheritance, money couldn't buy happiness, and it damn sure couldn't solve the problem of sheer loneliness or having to make every decision on my own. All I had was my sister Imani and my brother Dennis. I also had to accept that my twenty-nine-year-old sister was the oldest person in my family and that many times she didn't have all the answers, as well as the fact that my little brother's mental health was deteriorating by the day. Sadly, there was nothing I could do about it.

Tati didn't know how blessed she really was, and it was annoying the shit out of me. Not to mention, I was getting more and more turned off about how she had changed, completely succumbing to the current trend of thottery.

When I met Tati, she was a lady. Now, she was acting like a typical Instagram hoe, ready to show the entire world our bedroom.

Irritated, I stepped closer to her and grabbed her by both of her wrists forcefully.

I lasered in on her dark brown eyes, giving her a death stare. In the black of her pupils, I could see my broad shoulders strong neck, and the disappointment riddled on my face. I needed her to know how serious I was even so, I knew I had to be gentle.

"Tati, we're only twenty-two years old. We're both in college doing our thing. Stop stressing. Everything is going to fall in place at the perfect time."

Tati looked at me with a flat gaze as she twitched her lips. "Look, baby. You keep forgetting that you're twenty-two, and I'm twenty-six, soon to be twenty-seven. I'm not trying to work for anybody, and my degree in Early Childhood Education will only allow me to be a teacher and make peanuts. I'm trying to retire by thirty, and Only Fans will get me there. I'm already making ten thousand dollars a month without showing my face and promoting that it's me. Imagine if I stopped hiding and went full-fledged. I'd finally be able to match your fly baby," she squealed in an irritating and whiny baritone.

I ripped her hands off of me and walked toward the bathroom. This conversation was over. I was preparing for the most crucial season of my career — scout season. In the next few months, scouts from the Brooklyn Nets, Golden State, and Miami Heat would be in attendance.

Although I was interested in playing for the Lakers in honor of my favorite player, Kobe Bryant, I still wanted to show out and do my best. It was a personal goal of mine to get three offers and have my pick of the litter.

As I stepped into the bathroom, ready to hop in the shower, I heard Tati's footsteps approach.

"Baby, you understand where I'm coming from, right? The last thing I want you to think is that I'm with you because of your money. That's why I'm working so hard on my own," she pleaded, looking up at me.

I took my eyes off her and headed toward the shower. Ignoring her, I cut the faucet on, and water ran down the sprout, hitting the fancy granite tiles.

"That's the problem right there. You don't have to work hard. I thought I made that clear by showing you that I got you, but as always, there you go with the overthinking and trying to outdo me when I'm not even in competition with you," I chided, my eyes traveling from her face down to her body in disgust. "Get your ungrateful ass out of my face. I've got practice in an hour," I scoffed as I slid the shower glass door shut, blocking her out of my view and mind before turning my back to her and disappearing in the steam.

Practice was already going to be long. I didn't have time for Tati and her bullshit. Instead of enjoying the life that came with fucking with a young, rich nigga, all she did was complain. Plenty of young and older women would gladly appreciate the life I was providing without grumbling. Tati had better tighten up, or I may just have to explore my options. Trust me, I had many.

"GOOD D, Dice. Stick 'em! Stick 'em! remember to stay on that ass!" Coach George yelled out to me as I nudged my opponent in his side, delivering the smoothest defense known to man.

Coach George's voice echoed over us again as I tried to grab the ball from my opponent. "Jax, block 'em! block 'em!"

I hated when Coach yelled out instructions to both of us at the same time. It always confused me.

"It will be ten times louder when you're playing on the court. Stay in the game at all times," Coach George reminded us.

Sprinting forward, I side-swept the ball from Jax and hailed down the court, swishing the ball between each hand and under each leg. I took my last dribble, stepped back, and threw my hands up as I eyed my surroundings, certain this was my shot to end practice for the day. With my heart beating, I threw the ball, knowing I had this three-pointer in the bag. The ball swished around the hoop several times, causing my nerves to skyrocket until it fell into the basket.

"Good work, Dice! Good work, team! Reel it in!" Coach George hollered across the court. The entire team huddled toward the middle of the court, sweat beading from our heads and many of us breathing hard.

Coach George, a bald, stocky middle-aged man, circled the inside of our huddle, eyeing us all. Glancing down at the watch on his wrist, he bounced his head twice.

"It's late, and it's Friday, so y'all get out of here. I want you to know that I see and appreciate your hard work. You guys have been practicing like it's the playoffs, and trust me, it will pay off. So, for that, I'm letting you go early and allowing you to sleep in a little late tomorrow. Practice starts at noon instead of nine a.m."

The expression on our faces and the light in our eyes lit up the whole huddle as we all processed what he just said. Straightening his back, Coach stood erect.

"Now, this extra time I'm giving you is for rest and studying. Don't waste this time partying, drinking, or pigging out. Trust me, it will show in your performance. It's crunch time. We're a few months away from one of our biggest games, which is especially important if you're a junior or a senior. Don't fuck it up and have me, USC, or the Trojans out here looking bad," Coach George ranted, pacing around our huddle and eyeing us all carefully.

"You've got it?"

"We've got it, Coach!" we all yelled in unison.

"Good! You're dismissed. See you tomorrow at noon!"

Heading toward the locker room, my right-hand man on and off the court, Ace, nudged me in the side. "Are you still rolling with us to Hyde tonight? We've got a section and got to be there no later than ten p.m."

Just as Ace paused, my phone vibrated with a text from Tati.

Tati: *I've booked reservations at Flemings for us, baby. Dinner on me tonight. I hate when we fight so I just want to show you how much I appreciate you.*

Looking down at the phone, fumbling my fingers on the screen, I felt a sting on my arm.

"Bruh, you hear me? Are you rolling with us tonight or what? I've got your name down, and the promoter is expecting USC's star Trojan to show up," Ace reiterated.

I fumed, inhaling a deep breath as my eyes stayed fixated on Tati's text. I put my phone on silent, then looked up at Ace and held out my hand.

"Yeah, man, I'll be there."

Ace dapped me up. "Good looks. I'll pull up around nine p.m. to get you."

"I'm not finna be home, so I'll pull up on you or meet you there."

"Cool. We can pregame at the crib. See you later."

"All right, bro," I replied, watching Ace dart into the locker room.

Despite the fact that I was USC's star athlete, not just a basketball player but the MVP of the entire school, I rarely partied. I spent most of my time in the gym, in the books, or deep inside Tati's pussy. Having a girl kept me grounded, but it also had me losing myself a bit and missing out on all the fun that came with being a star player. That's exactly why I decided to ditch dinner with Tati and head out of the house before she got back. Considering that I knew her schedule like the back of my hand, I slid into the house, quickly dressed, and scrammed over to Ace's.

I had a few shots while Ace and our other boy, Lava, smoked some weed. When they tried to pass the blunt to me, I declined as always. Drugs were never my thing. I barely even drank. The only thing I cared about was making it to the NBA. Not that I needed the money. Like Tati said, I was loaded. However, since losing my parents and being away at school in LA, basketball was the only thing I had to look forward to apart from my only family, my sister and brother.

A QUARTER UNTIL TEN P.M., Ace, Lava, and I strolled out of the crib, hopped in my drop top Audi, and made our way to Hyde. The sun had set, and a cool breeze hit us as we drove down Selma Avenue. It felt damn good to finally get a break to kick it with my boys. As soon as we hopped out of the car, the valet took my keys, and we motioned toward the front of the line, bypassing those waiting outside and the paparazzi snapping pictures of a few celebrities.

"Dice Bleeker's here!" one of the male photographers announced, his British accent almost throwing me off.

Ace shielded me as I walked in. "Cool it. Dice isn't taking any interviews or photos, so fall back. You don't want us to have to get his lawyer involved," Ace warned as he and Lava stood their ground, allowing me to walk past the swarm of photographers.

"Good looks!" I praised Ace for handling the swarming paparazzi like a pro.

"You know I got you, bro," he replied as we headed toward the front door.

The tall, stout bouncer took one look at me, Ace, and Lava and let us in. Hyde Sunset was a small, exclusive venue, and although general admission wasn't allowed, it still boasted a large line of partygoers outside.

While I didn't party much, whenever I did get out, I only stepped foot in the best of the best spots where celebrities and athletes attended. Hyde was no different. Between its luxurious décor adorned with leather booths, an inviting ambiance, and world-renowned art, Hyde was one of the best spots to dine for lunch and party during the night. The best thing about it was that you could count on hobnobbing with LA's finest, considering that if you got into Hyde, you were a big deal.

As we got situated in our section, I eyed my surroundings. Across from me were a few influencer thots, and on the opposite corner stood YG and a gang of bitches. Almost all of them looked just like Kehlani. On the other end stood a few Russians, most likely fellow club owners in the city. Several minutes later, our bottles arrived, along with a few trays of appetizers. I dug into a chicken wing and cleaned it off its bone. Seconds later, our section became full of white and Asian bitches. Ace and Lava were having a blast as they sat sandwiched between two hoes, fondling and kissing each other.

Completely turned off, considering that I only had eyes for Black women, I downed a glass of Ace of Spades and stood up from the couch. Glancing around, every section looked the same, and every bitch looked the same. They wore their hair the same, the same cheap ass spandex clothing, and none of them were thick.

At that exact moment, I wished I stayed home with Tati. As the liquor settled into me, my mood changed. I was twenty-two years old, and I had all the money and access in the world, but a hole in my heart from my father losing his battle with MS and my mother committing suicide. It didn't matter how much I had. I always felt empty. Fighting tears, I grabbed the bottle of Ace and Spades and took it to the head.

As I gulped down the last remnants, my eyes traveled over the most alluring woman I'd seen all night.

There she was.

She was tall, cinnamon skin tone, with a physique so tight that you knew she was in the gym several days a week. While she wasn't exactly my type stature-wise, considering that I loved BBWs, she had a mature yet youthful aura that I appreciated. Her hair was cut short into a pixie cut, accentuating her long neck. Her outfit was modest yet sexy. Wearing an off-the-shoulder cream-colored blouse, her sexy, chiseled collarbone drew me in. She paired off her top with light blue denim jeans and wedges, intriguing me without having to look sleazy. *Confidence.*

As I admired her, she caught my eye and winked at me. Situated in a booth with three other mature-looking women who all carried themselves like ladies, my mystery crush walked away from her friends, never breaking eye contact with me. I stepped down from my section and headed in her direction until we met each other in the center.

Between the loud trap music and the squeals from the partiers, hearing her speak was nearly impossible. Still, as soon as our bodies touched, the feeling of our chests thumping against each other said more than we ever needed to utter. There was an enticing yearning in my heart to know everything about her, and from the soft twinkle in her eye, as she looked up at me, it was evident that the feeling was mutual.

young rich nigga

Charlene Moore

JUST FROM LOOKING AT HIM, I KNEW HE WAS YOUNG, yet there was something so damn familiar about the chemistry we shared. I couldn't deny it. I usually didn't care to meet men in the club, but we weren't at just any club. We were at Hyde, and if his young ass was in here, it was because he had some money and some status, which meant I had to know him. Still, the more and more I looked into his cognac-shaded eyes, the way he made me feel in his presence gave me the inclination that I already knew him pretty well.

"What's your name, gorgeous?" he whispered into my ear, his husky scent commanding my undivided attention.

I stood on my tippy toes, leaning forward to reach him despite the fact that I was wearing wedges. "Charlene. What's your name, handsome?"

"Darren. Darren Bleeker. But on the court, they call me Dice."

After introducing himself, I hopped back almost instantly, completely embarrassed. No wonder he felt familiar. He was more than familiar. *This fine, tall, young stout was the son of Bonita Bleeker, my ex-husband's mistress.* Worst of all was that before I found out that Bonita was fucking my late husband, we were all tight as thieves — me, Don, Bonita, and her husband, Rob. Aside from fucking my husband, cheating on hers, and sharing dick with her daughter, Bonita was a pretty decent mother. She and Rob ensured their kids were well taken care of, so much so that everyone in Atlanta knew the Bleeker kids were loaded due to the two hundred-million-dollar estate they inherited. Every single one of the kids was holding, especially Imani, who not only received money from Bonita and Rob, but half of my late husband Don's estate, as she was his goddaughter. Now, Imani was running several popular boutiques, along with a restaurant, and buying up tons of property to revitalize the west side of Atlanta. *Lucky little bitch.*

"What's wrong, baby?" Darren asked, interrupting my thoughts. Even he could sense the change in my energy.

"USC?"

"Yeah. That's a problem?"

"It is. You're just too young for me. I'm old enough to be your momma, boy," I declared, backing away from him.

He grabbed me by the arm so swiftly that I jerked forward, right into his chest, submerging into his laden scent.

"But you ain't my momma, and if what I feel is real, you just might be my lady," he asserted, his smooth baritone incepting its way into my soul.

Arrogant, confident, and smooth, just like my late ex-husband, Don. God rest his soul.

Just the certainty in his voice did it for me, chiseling down my spine, exciting my lady parts. I hadn't had a man step to me like that in a while.

Who was I kidding? He wasn't a man. He was a little ass boy that I actually watched grow up for the first few years of his life. Nonetheless, I'm sure he wouldn't recognize me initially, considering that Don and I were divorced by the time he was in grade school, and my connection to the Bleekers fizzled out.

I sucked my teeth and twisted my lip as my eyes danced up and down his profile. I couldn't take my eyes off his chestnut-coated skin, accentuating jawline and broad lips. I peered up at him, taking in his masculinity from his stacked shoulders, long neck, and strong arms. He was a baby by age but a man in sight. *Damn, this young nigga was fine.*

"How old are you?" I asked, breaking the sexual silence that danced between us.

"Old enough," he confidently shot back.

I squinched my eyes, trying to gauge my memory. I knew his sister, Imani, had to be close to thirty years old, which meant he was a few years younger, hopefully of legal age, at least. But there was no guarantee that Darren was twenty-one years old, considering I knew he had the money to pay off any club bouncer in the city to let him in, even if he was underage.

"Oh really?" I challenged him as I slowly and seductively bit my lips.

Truthfully, I had no idea that Darren was a star basketball player, and as much as I tried to fight it, I was impressed.

"Really. Now, how about we get out of here and go have dinner somewhere quieter where we can talk and get to know each other better?"

The slick sound of his tongue slapped against his wide, smooth lips as our eyes locked. He had no idea that not only did we know each other, but we were already connected in ways that made our sexual chemistry damn right scandalous. The pressing question was, how long would I allow this to go on before I revealed myself or before he put two and two together? Mischief lined the pit of my stomach as I smirked, allowing the scandal to dance around my mind.

"Flemings Steakhouse," I chided, determined to see just what kind of baller he was.

Was he the frugal, responsible kind, head equally in the game and in the books, or was he a young, rich nigga, not afraid to spend that shit?

A hint of hesitation painted his face once I said Flemings, but he quickly brushed it off. Since he had offered, he had better be ready to put his money where his mouth was. Grabbing my hand fully in his, he pulled me away without ever turning around to his friends. And when I think about it, I never once alerted my girls that I was sneaking off on a late-night getaway.

***

WATCHING Darren whip his drop-top Audi had me hot and ready like a box of Little Caesars pizza. I wasn't sure if it was the beating wind that had my nipples on rocks or if it was the pheromones oozing out his pores. Still, whatever it was, I was feeling it.

Don "Greedy" Davidson, the late heavyweight boxer, was my ex-husband, so I was used to luxury cars, exotic destinations, and five-star restaurants. Still, by the time I met Don, he was almost thirty and getting money for a long time. Darren wasn't a day older than puberty and was sitting on a hefty inheritance with a promising future. I couldn't believe he was turning me on this much.

"What do you want to hear, hunny?" Darren offered, with an eagerness to serve me.

"It's your world and your car, so play whatever you like."

Darren leaned over, his manly aroma massaging my senses, and planted a warm kiss on my cheek. "No, it's your world. Whatever you want, you get. Your wish is my command, baby."

I chuckled, and heat rose to my cheeks. At that moment, I knew I was blushing. I couldn't believe this little boy, who I watched grow up and younger than all three of my sons, was igniting this kind of fire in me. While he was young, his charming ways were reminiscent of my late husband, Don. Darren was smooth, tall, good-looking, with a broad stature that made me feel protected.

I nodded in agreement, then pursed my lips as I was at a loss for words. His young ass had me stumbling and shit. Before he even let me answer, a soft melody rang through the car, a soothing voice dancing in the air. The beat was reminiscent of the trendy Afrobeat sound that every DJ across the nation played.

A breathy baritone, repeating the words Casamigos several times, blasted from the stereo as Darren massaged the inside of my light denim jeans. His strong, powerful hands covered the base of my thighs as he gripped me tighter than I expected. Licking my lips slowly, I nestled back into the seat, determined to sit back, live in the moment, and enjoy every second with this young, rich nigga.

<hr>

TWENTY MINUTES LATER, Darren slid up the valet path of Flemings and put the car in park. He hopped out and beckoned to my side faster than the valet boy could even blink. Gentle yet firmly, Darren pulled my hand into his as he lifted me out of my seat. Crossing my legs, I found my step onto the curb and followed behind him. Without saying a word, he threw his keys to the valet and then winked his eye. To be so young, he carried himself like an old-school cat, especially in his mannerisms. While I didn't look my age at all, it was evident that I was on the mature side. With that said, I wondered if Darren adjusted himself and his behavior to impress me. Hmm. He knew he was dealing with a cougar. He may have been young, but he wasn't dumb.

Did I just call myself a cougar? Damn, I was really getting old.

I squinted my eyes, deliberately watching him from behind as he led me through the interior of the open-view, dimly lit restaurant. Nah, he wasn't forcing it. Between the smooth glide accentuating from his shoulders down to the sly bop driving from his hips as he took each step, his entire posture screamed grown man.

"Good evening. My name is Talley. Do you have reservations?" the young Japanese girl inquired, bouncing her gaze between both of us.

"Yeah, Tatiana Starks. The reservations were for eight p.m., though."

The hostess scrolled through an iPad, tipping her head up and down as her eyes followed along the screen. "I'm afraid that your reservation was taken, and unfortunately, we just closed our dining room. If you'd like, you and your date can enjoy dinner and drinks at the bar."

"Sure, that's cool," Darren affirmed as we followed the hostess toward the cream-colored, marble-top bar.

"Enjoy your evening."

The hostess and I exchanged smiles until she turned her back to walk away. Now facing Darren, I watched his veins pop out his arm as he pulled my chair out.

Damn, he was fine, fine! And a gentleman, at that.

As I plopped down on the bar stool, admiring the fuzzy

romance ridden on the faces of several couples, I was startled by a screeching echo.

"Dice! What's up?" an annoying nasally voice belted from the throat of an overweight Hispanic chick dressed as a server.

Darren turned around quickly. "Hey, Sheena. How you doing?"

With her hand on her hip and a raised eyebrow, she sniffled. "I'm good. Where's Tati? I thought you two had reservations tonight."

This was the second time I had heard the name Tati. She had to be his girlfriend. While I would never sit through this kind of bullshit with a man my age, I made a pass for Darren. Come on, we just met, and there's no way his fine, sexy ass didn't have a girlfriend. Not only was he attractive, but he was also a star athlete, so it was to be expected.

"Tati's probably at the house. I'm actually not really sure, but I do hope you have a great evening," he politely replied, dismissing her. *Dominant without losing his cool.*

Just from the surety in his voice, my panties began to moisten, and my nipples brushed against my blouse, hardening as a result. From the looks of Sheena's tightened scowl, she was startled, taken aback, or possibly offended. Nonetheless, she walked away without responding, which I was grateful for, and I'm sure Dice was, too.

Biting my bottom lip and sucking it in with my tongue, I chuckled. "So you leave your girlfriend in the house to take me out to the same spot that you stood her up for dinner?"

I had to pull his card. Mr. Smooth Operator was going to have to face me head-on after I sat through that awkward situation. To my surprise, Darren softly chuckled, grabbing my hand into his as he sucked me into his fervent gaze.

"She's always there, but you..." He paused and licked his lips, then rubbed them against each other slowly and methodically. "...You're a butterfly, meaning if I didn't catch you, you'd easily fly away, which I couldn't risk happening."

Damn. He was good.

"You know just what to say, don't you?"

Licking his lips profusely, he smirked. "I do."

"I see," I flirted back, trying my best to conceal my nervousness, but I could feel my eye twitching. Between Darren's aroma and the way confidence radiated on him, he had me intrigued.

"I appreciate you holding your composure despite shawty interrupting us. You're mature. I like that."

Of course, I'm mature. I'm old enough to be yo' momma.

"No problem. I wouldn't expect a baller like you to be single."

"Well, I'm not married, so according to the law, I am single." Scanning me from the neck down, his eyes lit up at my bare hands. "And I don't see any ring on your finger, so you're single, too. So we're good?" He nibbled on his bottom lip, slowly undressing me with his eyes. I could feel the heat between us.

I nodded in agreement. "We're good," I said, twisting my lips, my eyes low, gazing over Darren slowly, and sizing him up from his feet until I settled on his crotch. I just knew his young ass was packing and had some stamina on him, not to mention he had money. I had definitely hit the jackpot all in one.

Clearly, I wasn't the only one feeling lucky. Winking his eye, Darren tickled my chin with his index finger. The firmness of his touch traveled up my arm to my collarbone, sending shocks down my spine. Before I knew it, Darren was grabbing my face into his, pulling me in with his warm, moist tongue, which I allowed because I couldn't help it, and shit, as a grown woman, I didn't owe anybody any explanations or apologies. I was in LA, and you know what they say, what happens in the wild, wild west, stays in the wild, wild west, and I for damn sure was going to enjoy myself.

superwoman

Imani

"THIS SHIT GETTING OUT OF HAND, MA. Something's got to give," Rugga, my boyfriend of three years, complained as he leaned against the entrance of our bedroom door inside our modernized new home in Marietta.

Biting my lip, I swallowed an exasperated breath as I contemplated what Rugga was asking me to do. It was just out of the question.

"Babe, you know I respect your feelings, but this is my baby brother you're talking about." I tried reasoning.

Stepping closer to me, Rugga took a deep breath, puffing his chest out, as his broad diaphragm pressed through his white cotton t-shirt. Long, lean, dark-skinned with beautiful dreadlocks down his back, Rugga had that New York swag I loved. A refined gangster turned luxury real estate tycoon, Rugga, came into my life at a time when I needed him most.

Pulling my hands into his, I caught a whiff of his classic, regal scent cloaked with Baccarat cologne. "Imani, Dennis is not a baby. He's eighteen years old. It's time for the little nigga nuts to hang. He needs his own spot ASAP! Between the pacing back and forth all night to that nasty ass stench in his room, this shit is getting out of hand," he asserted, using his hands to enforce his posture, Black man essence oozing off of him.

I sucked my lips in, inhaling a deep breath of aggravation, and slowly exhaled. "Baby, Dennis is not ready for that level of responsibility. Besides, I'm all he has. *We're* all he has," I iterated. "Darren's in school in LA, and you know we're estranged from our grandparents. I can't just abandon him." The hollowness of my voice alone sounded like I was pleading rather than defending my brother's honor.

Almost instantaneously, Rugga grabbed me into his arms, his firm embrace hugging me into submission as he towered over my small, petite frame. Raising my chin in the air with his finger forced me to look into his darting, protective eyes. Being single for two years after losing my father to MS, my mother, and my child's father to suicide, and dealing with all the deceit of our love triangle, I had severe trust issues. Since Rugga came into my life, I learned how to let my guard down as I grew to depend on him.

As his big, powerful hands caressed my back, pulling me deeper into him, my defenses disappeared. Rugga meant well and was just being my man, looking out for my best interests, which I could admit he did a great job at.

"You won't be abandoning him. You can still meal prep for him, go shopping for him, and do his laundry if that's what you choose to do. Shit, he can even come over every week for Sunday dinner, but he can't stay here. It's taking a toll on you," he insisted, his raspy voice rugged like a gritty sidewalk, which equally enticed and intrigued me at the same time.

Poking my lips out, with my hands now on my hips, I shook my head back and forth. "You make it sound so bad that I take care of my brother." I pouted, avoiding his gaze and fuming toward the wall.

Rugga kissed his teeth, and the crack, snapple, and pop flew out of his mouth abruptly before he snickered loudly.

"Nah, I ain't gon' let you do that. You know damn well that YOU," Rugga pointed at me with an accusatory finger, "make it sound so bad that you take care of Dennis. You're always complaining about how tired you are. Imani, the truth is that we don't have the manpower or time to take care of Dennis. Not between us running three boutique locations, taking care of Zion, and my real estate firm together. We don't have the time to babysit yo' brother."

As I fidgeted in his arms, trying to shake him off, I knew he was right. I was tired, and dealing with Dennis and his bipolar depression worsening day by day wasn't making it any easier. I rolled my eyes, kissed my teeth, and looked down at the cream-colored marble tiles beneath my feet. Unlike Darren and I, Dennis took our parents' death the hardest, and I was responsible for picking up the pieces by making sure that both of my brothers were good. I became their momma, making sure Darren was settled into USC, and that Dennis continued to attend high school, which was the hardest of the two.

"Baby, I know we don't have the time, but if I don't do it, who will?"

"I'm not saying we have to cut him off. I'm just simply saying he needs his own space. The little nigga isn't in school. He's not taking his meds, and as your man, I can't sit by and watch him abuse you, but I can find him something nice and manageable in the area so he's close to us. We can take turns checking on him during the week. Trust me, baby, everything will be fine."

Gripping me tighter, the cut above his lip deepened as I gazed into his eyes. He knew the scar was one of my favorite features about him because it displayed his silent strength and sex appeal. I pouted, steam fuming from my mouth because I wanted to fight him so badly on this, but I couldn't.

"Alright, find the place. I'll talk to Dennis and his therapist."

"Good," Rugga stated as he lifted me off the ground.

Wrapping my legs around him, I sat comfortably at his waist as he held me up with his powerful hands.

"Now, since I've let you have your way, you better let me have mine," I flirted, twirling my tongue around my lips.

"Come on, baby, I don't have time. I have a meeting at Phipps Plaza in an hour, and don't you have to be at the boutique in a few?"

With my lip twisted, I rolled my eyes. "Baby, did you

forget that we're the bosses? We make our own schedules. Now, I need you to do that thang that I like, real bad," I cooed into his ear, nibbling on his neck.

Rugga's dick instantly rose to attention, and his growl turned into a sly smirk before he motioned toward the bed, threw me down, and wrestled me out of my robe. With my legs cocked open, he spread his nose along my clit, taking in my natural scent before spreading his tongue across my pussy. Slowly, he thrust his two fingers inside my wet plum until he hit the back of my uterus and began pulsing in and out, all while sucking on my throbbing clit simultaneously. In bliss, I held my head back, savoring every moment, delighted to escape the daunting reality I would soon face.

AFTER AN HOUR-LONG SESSION OF LOVEMAKING, I finally got myself together for the day. I hated leaving the house after eleven a.m., as it reminded me that the morning was already gone, but some things couldn't wait. Sex helped me decompress and gave me the patience to handle stress, so it was a must daily, sometimes even twice a day. As I fixed the collar on my silk blouse and situated my oversized bag across my arm, making my way down the steps, a poignant stench slapped my nose. It grew stronger and stronger with each step I descended. Sucking my teeth so hard caused the smell to invade my mouth, producing a nasty loud cough. I dug into the bottom of my bag until I found a mask and covered my face. Not only was COVID back on the rise, but I made it a habit to always wear masks whenever I entered Dennis' room. It was needed.

Without knocking, I turned the knob and was met by a dozen soda cans, six Casamigos bottles, and several beer cans spread out across the floor. I tried not uto fume so I wouldn't inhale the musk that permeated the room. Irritated, I kicked the bottles out of my way, approaching Dennis, who sat with his back turned to me, a headset on his head, staring at his TV. I got close up on him and slapped the hell out the back of his fat neck, his skin blubbering across my hand.

Immediately, he threw his headset off, stood, and faced me. Overweight, and tall with a slumped posture and a curved neck, Dennis struggled to even stare at me.

"What the fuck, Imani?" he barked. "You know I don't like it when you sneak up on me.." His words were slurring as usual, which became a signature part of his speech within the last year.

Dennis had become an all-out alcoholic and addict. He was addicted to three things: sugar, liquor, and Percocet. Sadly, all three of them had aged him terribly. At only eighteen years old, he looked at least forty.

"Dennis, I'm trying really hard to be gentle with you, but this shit has gotten way out of hand. It's Monday, nearly noon, and you smell like shit. Clean this room the fuck up and take a fucking shower!"

Dennis snorted, kissing his teeth. "I'll do it later," he muttered as he turned his back on me, hobbled forward, and picked up his headset.

In the next second, a racking beat blasted from the

speakers as Trippie Redd, Dennis' favorite artist, rang through the room. Banging his head and fumbling with the keys on his game controller, Dennis squealed out as he sang along to the devilish words and dark ambiance that followed as soon as the music started.

"Dennis, I'm serious. Don't let me come back today, and you haven't cleaned up this shit!"

"Yeah, yeah, yeah, whatever," he sang, following the tune of the wretched bullshit he blasted in my house on the regular.

I felt my blood pressure rising as I exhaled an aggravated breath and turned around to exit. Shaking my head, I stormed out of the house and headed to my car. Thank God for the refreshing Georgia air that whisked the terrible smell from Dennis' room out of my nostrils.

THIRTY MINUTES LATER, I walked through Vivid Couture, the hottest boutique with the chicest, most stylish garments in the city. In just four short years, Vivid Couture was doing amazing, with three stores scattered across the metro Atlanta area, with this location being its flagship store, bringing in a half million dollars each quarter. Considering I owned the three buildings we operated out of overhead was down, and profit margins were up.

Soft music belted through the store, accompanied by a clean jasmine scent, Vivid Couture's signature fragrance. I strolled past the two cashiers, checking out customers and a few personal stylists on the floor, grabbing pieces. They all smiled in my direction, and I nodded, pleased that the store was moderately full on a Monday afternoon.

I dashed toward the back and headed to my office area, startled by TT, my best friend, and Vivid Couture's creative manager. With AirPods in his ears and his fingers typing a mile a minute on the computer, TT's eyes lit up when he saw me.

"Thanks. Got to go. I'll call you back!" he iterated before taping his AirPods and glowing with a smile.

"Hello, miss lady. I see you finally decided to stroll into work."

I dropped my two bags onto the floor and rolled my eyes at TT's flamboyant ass, who was dressed to the gods today, wearing a yellow and black polka dot blouse with black skinny slacks and a matching yellow scarf. His skin shined brighter than a strip of mustard on a hotdog.

"Don't fuss with me. This morning was hell. Well, that was after my two very much-needed orgasms." I snickered.

"Woe is the millionaire who gets wonderful, consistent dick from a man she actually loves."

"Somebody sounds like they're hating."

"Duh! Who doesn't wish they had your life, Ms. Bleeker? You're doing the damn thing hunny!"

I smiled, sunk down into my chair, and exhaled. TT was one of the few people that could change my mood from sucky to jovial. He was a great friend, a wonderful business partner, and always bigged me up, even when I felt my lowest. Thinking back to Dennis' condition dampened my spirits as I felt my smile turning into a shallow frown.

"Aht-aht. Pick your face up, sis. What's going on?" he quizzed as he got up from his seat and rushed to my side.

"Nothing," I lied.

TT sucked his teeth so fast. "Girl, please. I know that face. It's not nothing, so tell me what the fuck is going on!"

Rolling my eyes, I faced him and exhaled. "It's Dennis."

TT chuckled. "What's going on with Mr. Roblox?"

With a hanging head and a caved-in chest, I took shallow yet audible breaths. "Rugga wants him to move out, and I agreed, but he's not ready. His condition is worsening, and although there is nothing I can do for him, kicking him out won't help either."

TT's grimace quickly softened as he stood, hovering over me with compassionate eyes.

"How bad is he?"

"Real bad. He's not showering. He's drinking excessively and eating terribly, and he hasn't been to therapy in a month. I don't know what to do, TT."

I looked up at him, then watched him bend to his knees to get eye level with me as I sat on the chair. He picked up my hand and caressed it.

"Babe, I know how much you love your brother, but I'm afraid you just can't be his Superwoman this time. He has to fight his demons on his own. Now, you can be there to assist, but you have to create some healthy boundaries, and the first one will be separating yourself. I agree with Rugga. Dennis has to move out unless he's going to drive you crazy."

My eyes watered as I listened to my best friend, who I knew had my best interest at heart, even deeper than

Rugga. TT had been around for years. He knew my entire family and had watched Darren and Dennis grow up. He knew, even more than Rugga, how badly Dennis' condition had affected me. He knew how much I struggled with depression after losing my parents and Don, and he witnessed me pick myself up time and time again. If anyone knew, TT, his twin sister Shima and my other best friend Crissy did. I was so grateful for the three of them who helped me run my business and raise my son, Zion. It felt knowing I had a village that genuinely cared for me because doing it all was becoming quite exhausting.

triggered

Dice

THE SUN HIT MY FACE, WAKING ME FROM MY slumber as I rolled over to find my wonder woman lying softly beside me. With flawless skin, a beauty mole under her nose, and soft freckles, she was aging gracefully, and everything about her turned me on. I would have never guessed that she was really fifty-four years old. From how soft her skin appeared to her natural aroma, well-manicured nails, and pedicured feet, it was evident that Charlene was well-kept and used to being taken care of, which explains her former marriage to a pro boxer. Women like her screamed wifey material. She just had that sauce that made a nigga want to take care of her every need. And it seemed like I was falling right in line.

It had been three days since I had been home, and every second, outside of Saturday morning practice, I spent with Charlene, whom I preferred to call Charla. The crispy buttermilk catfish she fried to perfection, creamy mashed potatoes, and savory collard greens she whipped up put me on my ass. After she rode me to orgasm, sucked me into a daze, and fed me these last few days, I can't lie. A nigga was open. She catered to me in every way, mentally stimulating me, listening to me, relaxing me, massaging my feet, allowing me some much-needed rest, just to wake up to her again preparing breakfast. All yesterday, we spent hours talking and bingeing our favorite show, *Suits,* on USA. Being with her felt easy, and we had so much in common. She had me forgetting that I was in a whole relationship with another woman, well, a girl, 'cause Tati ain't have shit on her.

In fact, Tati had been blowing up my phone nonstop to the point that I had to block her number. I didn't care what the fuck she had going on because my mind was only on how I was going to get Charlene to stay in LA for the next few months. I needed her by my side to finish out the playoffs. Her wisdom, advice, and how comfortable I felt with her had me ready to put her up in a condo, all expenses covered, just so I could be close to her.

I slipped out of the bed, careful not to wake my sleeping beauty. However, I failed as I watched her body stir, causing her to turn over.

"Good morning, baby," she spoke, her voice soothing and alluring. "What are your plans for the day?"

Leaning forward, she crawled on her knees to the edge of the bed and pecked me softly on the lips. The look in her eyes warmed my heart.

"Good morning, babe. I have class and practice today."

"No worries. My flight leaves in a bit, so I'll be out of your hair shortly," she replied casually and dainty-like.

"No, it doesn't, and you don't gotta go nowhere."

Her brow raised as she snickered and licked her lips. "What did you do, Dice?"

"Stay with me in LA until I finish the playoffs and graduate."

Charla's cheeks filled out as a blush of rose shadowed her face. "Dice, as flattered as I am, I can't stay in LA. I've got—"

"What? You don't work? Your sons are out of the house. You don't own any pets, and you can monitor your home through the Ring camera app. What's stopping you from being with me?" I dared her as I stood up erect with my arms folded.

Pausing with a smile, Charla's eyes beamed. "Everything. You don't think we're moving a bit fast?"

I loudly laughed as I shook my head. "I ain't asking for your hand in marriage. I just want you to spend the next two or three months with me."

Standing up with her knees plastered on the bed, she folded her arms. "Why? Why me?"

"You know why," I chided.

She blushed. "I need to hear you say it," she demanded.

I grabbed her hands in mine. "You're smart and experienced, and I know it's only been a few days, but I trust you, and I trust that you'll have my best interest at heart, especially as it relates to these NBA contracts and just navigating overall," I confessed.

"So, you think I'm your manager?" she asked as she hopped out of the bed and placed her hands on her hips.

"Nah, ma, it's not like that. I just value your opinion, and I appreciate your company. Tell the truth, when's the last time you've driven up the hills in Malibu singing your heart out and chasing stars? Don't front. You know you feel it, too."

She sucked her teeth. "Let me find out I got your young ass sprung off this cougar cat!" She giggled.

"I'm Dice Bleeker, baby. I done had enough pussy. Trust me, this ain't that!"

"So, what is it?" she challenged me.

I was tired of Charla being difficult, so I grabbed her forcefully, taking a handful of her ass as I bit down hard on my bottom lip. She wouldn't give up quizzing me, so I had to make it flavorful, although the truth was that she reminded me so much of my mother. She was mature and knowledgeable, and she made me feel safe. It was hard trusting girls my age because I knew they were out for my money, status, and fame. Charla wasn't after any of that. Shawty had her own and a lot to teach me.

"It's just a vibe I can't explain, and I don't wanna lose it without exploring it to its fullest if that makes sense."

Charla twisted her lips and rolled her eyes. "I guess it does, and I guess you're right. Nothing is stopping me from staying here with you."

"Good, because trust me, I'm gon' take care of you, mami. Whatever you want. Whatever you need, I got you."

She nodded as she wiggled her soft ass on my crotch. I tried to control myself, but my dick couldn't stay down.

Charla smirked as she looked down at my shaft, poking through my briefs. Without a word, she dropped to her knees and swallowed me whole. Her warm mouth grabbed me in as my dick hit the back of her wet throat. Bobbing and weaving her head, the gawky sounds of pleasure filled my ears as I floated away in paradise. With a soaking wet mouth, she twisted and twisted both hands around my dick as she pulsed her head back and forth.

"Shit," I cursed as I opened my eyes, catching my balance before tumbling back.

Charla had me in another dimension that, before I knew it, she sucked the nut out of me, leaving me depleted.

"Enjoy your day, baby. Text me what you want for dinner, and I'll have it ready for you later."

As my breath began to recover, I motioned toward the closet and pulled out a black duffel bag. I opened it slightly to view its contents and ensure it was the right bag before tossing it toward Charla. "There's twenty thousand cash in there. Get whatever you want, mamas. I'll Cash App you the money for dinner. While you're at it, find a few condos in the city you'd like to stay in. I want us out of this suite no later than next week."

Charla's eyes beamed, and a hint of blush sprang up her cheeks as fast as a helium balloon. "Okay, baby. I'll get on it," she replied as she stood on her tippy toes and kissed me. Before she walked away, I smacked her hard on the ass, and she giggled.

"You nasty boy, you nasty!"

That I was.

⸻

Strolling through Leavey Library feeling, looking, and smelling like a king, with that cougar scent all over me, I made my way to a quiet area. Heads down and shoulders crunched in books, eyes scrolling laptops, and ears filled with AirPods, Leavey was relatively quiet for the mid-afternoon. I had about an hour to double-check my research paper before class started. Seeing as I was graduating in less than three months, my workload was full of research and final projects. As I settled into the seat and pulled my laptop out of my book bag, I was met by a loud, annoying grunt.

"So, you go MIA, don't come home for days, block my number, then show up on campus like everything's sweet?" Tati roared, her voice hoarse and the sides of her lips crusted with white foam. Not to mention, she was wearing a bonnet and a skimpy two piece set she normally pranced around the house in.

Considering the high I was on from my extended weekend with Charla, not even an argument with Tati's thot ass could fuck my mood up. Staring blankly as my arms hung limply at my sides, I reached for her hand. Instantly, she slapped my hand off of her.

"Tati, we need to talk, but not—"

Tati's neck jerked as she placed her hands on her hips. "But not here? Then where? At our home that you've abandoned the last few days, leaving me to wonder where the fuck you've been at?"

Nothing about Tati's pitch represented an inside voice.

Boisterous and screeching, Tati didn't give a fuck that several eyes were blinking, accompanied by sudden head shaking and raised eyebrows. I lifted my head, searching the level above us, and noticed two students hunched over the ledge staring down at us.

"Quiet down, Tati!"

With pursed lips, a menacing scowl, and her arms now folded, Tati fumed, breath humming from her mouth. "No! You embarrassed the fuck out of me by taking another bitch on the dinner reservations I made for us, yet now you're so worried about our business getting out?"

Rubbing my hands together as I licked my lips profusely, something I did when I was exceptionally nervous, I reached forward to grab Tati by the wrists again. There was no way that I was going to have it out with her in front of everybody. Tati knew what a spectacle like this could do to my reputation, and yet she still didn't give a fuck.

Her red eyes were full of rage, her nostrils flared, and her chest slowly pulsing as she shouted, incoherency belting from her mouth. I couldn't make out a word she was saying. Her outburst gnawed at my nerves as she repeatedly shouted the same words.

"So, who's the bitch, Darren? Who's this bitch you're fucking? Who's the old cougar bitch you took to Flemings instead of me? Oh, you ain't think Sheena wasn't gon' tell me? Who is the bitch?" she yelled as she raised her cell phone to my face.

It was a picture of Charlene and me kissing.

Scraping my teeth together, I deeply inhaled before

storming past her. Tati was way out of line. Not only was she loud as fuck and embarrassing, but the seething hatred in her eyes also bothered me to the core. With that look, it wouldn't surprise me if Tati weren't planning to do something really fucking stupid that could hurt Charlene. Just the thought of Tati's potential malice had me on edge. I quickened my step, trying to belt out of the library, but Tati was right behind me.

"Where the fuck are you going, Darren? Answer me! Who the fuck is this old bitch you're fucking? She looks old enough to be your fucking mother. You sick bastard."

At the word mother, I lost it. I turned around on my heel and snatched Tati's phone out of her hand. I threw it down on the floor before stomping on it. Tati's slack expression and quietness shocked me more than my behavior. Yoking her by the neck, with my chin locked, I whispered, "Don't you ever, and I mean ever, mention my mother again, bitch. And don't bother going back to the condo. The locks will be changed."

I released my grip around her neck as we stood in front of the library's entrance. The only feeling I had in my heart for Tati was disgust and hatred. As tears filled her eyes and began to fall from the sides of her face, she sniffled several times.

"Where am I supposed to go?"

With a sneer on my lips, I bounced my shoulders. "Wherever the fuck your OnlyFans money can afford!"

As I turned my back on Tati, leaving her standing in the library, I couldn't help but notice the circle of bystanders watching on, some with their phones out recording and others with a sense of awe riddled on their faces. I shook my head, irritated, knowing that I'd have to explain myself to not only Coach George but my boys and my team. Hopefully, there wouldn't be any harsh repercussions. Either way, I'd take it on the chin because Tati was way out of line, and there was no way, I wasn't going to check her ass.

CHAPTER FIVE

crushin' on a young'n

Charlene

Steam from the brewing hot tea soothed my throat as I swallowed a gulp while jotting down notes on the legal pad to the right of me. The fine cashmere silk rug sat beneath my feet, warming my toes as the chilling air circulated throughout the quiet room. Tina, my financial advisor, was rattling off my expenses for the last three months for our quarterly review. Although she provided an electronic copy for me to download, I still preferred to write the numbers down. It was just something about penning the stroke of a money sign attached to each number that made it real for me, especially since I became solely responsible for all of my finances. It became even more real once Don passed.

Tina's raspy voice echoed through the screen of my MacBook, bringing my wandering mind back to the center.

Her sharp collarbone peeked over the oval-lined powdered pink chiffon blouse lying against her fawny skin.

"You're doing pretty well with keeping your expenses minimized and consistent, which is a good thing..."

"But?" I knew that lingering sigh in Tina's breath meant that she had more to say but was trying to sweeten it up for me. "Just say it," I demanded.

Pressing the palms of her hands together, she sighed. "No amount of budgeting will supplement the fact that you have no real income. Over the last few years, you've been pinching off the spousal support Don left you, which leaves your liquid cash balance at seven hundred and thirty-eight thousand dollars. The retirement fund you've been saving sits at three million dollars, but the way inflation is, your lifestyle, and how long you have to go until retirement, that amount is simply a drop in the bucket." Tina paused, exhaling dramatically and gritting her teeth as if the words she was about to speak were life-changing. "You have to find a way to bring in some consistent income without making any high-risk investments, Charlene," Tina stressed.

I let out an exasperated breath as I shifted my eyes from the computer screen to the window of the luxury suite Darren and I had hidden in the last few days. As I looked over the perfectly made bed, Darren's gym bag in the corner, three Rolex watches, and a few rings sitting along the nightstand around the entire room, taking in the fact that I was laid up with this young ass boy all these days. Meanwhile, I had real shit to deal with. My lip turned up in disgust at myself. I was too fucking old for this shit. While I wasn't broke, I'd be struggling in retirement if I didn't devise a plan to bring in some serious cash. Tina was right.

"Charlene, you're only fifty-four. You're still young. There's a lot you can do that's low risk. Real estate, for example. You can sell homes or start wholesaling. You can start a business or write a book. You can get married again so that your husband can cover your living expenses. Getting married again would help you at least preserve your finances if you don't decide to return to work."

"Work? Tina, you must have forgotten who you're talking to. I haven't worked since 1994." Although I had a court reporter's license and a bachelor's degree, I only used it for a few months before Don and I married. After fifteen years, we divorced in 2011, and I'd been taken care of ever since. I had a great alimony package, including child support, that I used to take care of my three sons, who are all self-sufficient at the very least. The rest I spent on maintaining the lifestyle Don introduced me to. Luckily, I knew how to save and invest my money, but bringing in money was never my strong suit. Not that I couldn't do it. I just never had to, so wrapping my mind around working now would be a big adjustment.

"Well, if you don't want to work, I suggest getting remarried at the very least. Marrying the right man can open a lot of doors for you. Have you ever thought about acting? Reality TV? Even without getting married, I'm sure there's a spot somewhere for you on *The Real Housewives of Atlanta*. You were married to Greedy Davidson."

Lightbulbs went off in my head. Tina's advice was golden. Getting married again to another hot athlete was the answer to my financial woes, and getting there would be a breeze and a treat. I bit down hard on my lip, full of excitement, as I got up from my seat and began pacing back and forth in front of the coffee table, my computer sat on.

Dice was already open, wanting me to stay with him for a few months. I knew how to get a ring out of a nigga. That wasn't a problem, as it seemed like he wanted me to be his manager already. Seeing as I was getting older, this time around with an athlete, I needed to build myself a career. It wasn't just enough to get my bills paid and my lifestyle afforded. I needed to build a real income through my association, and if I had to put in a little work, that was fine, especially because Dice was young with a promising future and could be molded. Unlike Don, Dice trusted me because, in his mind, I was experienced, and I knew that his trust would get me very far. I also knew he was looking for a mother figure in his woman, and I was prepared to tug on those emotional wounds to ensure I got what I wanted.

First, I had to test his commitment, which started with a small task.

"Charlene! Are you there?"

I jolted back to the coffee table and turned my computer screen forward. "Yeah, I'm here, just thinking. You might be right. I do have a wealthy friend that I'm seeing right now. I've been in LA with him this past week. He asked me to stay with him for a few months and offered to get a condo for us to stay in. I will ask him to buy me a villa overseas as an investment property while he's at it."

Tina poked her lips out and nodded slowly. "A vacation

property is a great investment. I have a real estate friend with properties in Jamaica, Panama, and Barbados. I'll send you a few options to present to him."

"Thanks, Tina. I appreciate it."

"No problem. Just remember that even though vacation villas are a great real estate investment, they still require maintenance fees, property taxes, and more. You'll need a business or housing manager. Are you ready for that type of work and expense?"

"No. But my man's gonna make it so easy for me to manage, so I'm not worried."

Tina's face lit up as she kissed her teeth and rubbed her hands together. The bling from her gigantic wedding ring nearly blinded me through the screen. When I first hired Tina, it was because she was on her third wealthy husband, and she used their money to grow into a multi-million dollar fortune. She also dedicated her work's mission to teaching women about financial literacy. She was a girl's girl, but most importantly, she understood the power of money and how to leverage it.

"I know that's right. Now, would you say this wealthy friend of yours is husband material?" Tina quizzed.

With a lightness in my chest, I grinned widely, laughter belting from my throat. "Definitely." I bubbled.

"GIRL, the way you ghosted us this past weekend, let's call you Casper. What's going on? Are you flying back to Atlanta with us tomorrow?" Shavonne, my good homegirl, asked as we sipped cocktails at Perch LA, my favorite rooftop in the city.

Straw from the bamboo seats pressed against my butt as I leaned back into the chair, taking in my surroundings. The clear skyline made way for the moderate breeze that shivered along my neck. I lifted my shoulders to combat the chilly air before fanning myself and giggling.

"Nah. I think I will stay in LA for the next few months with my friend."

Shavonne sat her drink down on the end table between us. "What friend?"

I bit my lip and paused as I thought about whether I should reveal the truth. Shit, what did I have to lose? Besides, I needed someone to rationalize this shit out that I had brewing with Darren. Things were moving so fast, and what I considered doing next needed to be discussed.

I placed my drink down and sat up straight in my seat before speaking. "I reconnected with someone. He's much younger, but he's balling girl, and he wants me to stay with him out here for the next few months."

Shavonne's brows crunched inward, and her lip protruded up. "Huh? Girl, what? Who is this nigga, and how young is much younger? And when you say balling, what do you mean? Is he Nick Cannon young and balling or Souljah Boy young and balling?" she inquired.

"Bitch, don't ever insult me. Souljah Boy is not balling."

Shavonne snickered, her laugh deepening as her smile widened. "Well, who the fuck is he?"

"His name is Darren Bleeker. He's the MVP at USC for

the Trojans. He graduates this year and has several deals on the table from the NBA."

Shavonne shimmied her shoulders, bouncing forward as she slapped her knee. "Okay, bitch. The NBA is different for you, but still a big bag."

"Bitch, a major bag, and he's already got it before even signing."

Shavonne tilted her head down and gave me a puzzled stare. "They gave him an advance already?"

"Nah. Darren is sitting on an inheritance."

"How big?" Shavonne reached forward for her glass and took a quick sip.

"A little under one hundred million."

Shavonne's eyes widened as she stretched her neck forward. Her large ears perked up, waiting to take in my latest gossip. "Bitch, what? Oh, you really hit the jackpot."

I nodded twice and twisted up my lips. "Although I shouldn't be telling you this, I know your nosey ass wasn't gon' stop until you got the drop on him yourself, so there's no point in omitting or hiding anything from you."

Shavonne raised her glass and leaned forward. I followed, picking my glass up until we met in the middle and clanked our drinks together. "You already know bitch. So spill it. I can tell you're brewing on more tea," she giggled.

"Girl, I'm fucking Don's mistress' son!"

"Wait! Bonita's son?" Shavonne inquired as she looked over her shoulders, eyeing the nearly empty bar as if we were discussing some top-secret news.

"Yeah, girl and his little young ass is open. He gave me twenty grand to go shopping this morning!"

"Damnnnnn. Baby boy got it like that. It's definitely safe to call you a cougar now. Over there putting that seasoned pussy on that young boy. You should be ashamed of yourself," Shavonne hissed, her sass overpowered by our laughs.

"I know I shouldn't be putting it on him like that, but mostly, I shouldn't even be feeling his young ass like this," I sighed sheepishly, trying my best to hide the smirk that was creeping up the corner of my mouth.

"Ahh, sookie sookie now. Don't tell me you're crushing on the young'n," Shavonne chided, her melody as if she were singing.

I licked my lips, thinking about how Darren and I fucked all night, round for round. He had the stamina of a champion, able to compete with a fifty-plus-year-old horn ball like me. His thick shaft was a tall magic stick, perfect for me to ride to the highest heights at the fastest speeds. The smoothness of the tip of his dick repeatedly knocked on my G-spot until I came over and over, my creamy pussy oozing with ecstasy. I bit my bottom lip, completely enthralled in a full porno flick in my head that I almost forgot Shavonne was sitting across from me.

"Yeah, you're feeling him. That little nigga gon' be yo' man. Watch and see." Shavonne folded her arms and pressed back into her seat. Repeatedly bouncing her head, she chanted, "Uh-huh. Uh-huh."

I couldn't fight a word she was saying because, in my sickly, overly excited mind, Darren was already mine.

CHAPTER SIX

Dice

MY STOMACH DROPPED INTO THE PITS OF MY SHOES as I watched my future slip away for the thirtieth time. The video of me choking Tati had gone so viral throughout USC's entire campus that special GIFs and memes were trending all over USC's Twitter tag. This was by far the most ridiculous one. Holding the phone in my hand, I watched a WWE SmackDown battle with my face plastered on Chris Brown's body, pounding the shit out of Tati, who was slapped atop Rihanna's frame. The jarring sound effects mimicking the thrash of lashes blared through my AirPods. My heart was thumping, and it felt like my blood was boiling. For the last two hours, I watched every video, pretending I wasn't seeing countless calls and texts from my teammates, coach, and other friends.

I took a deep breath, trying to gather my thoughts

before entering the suite. From outside the door, I could smell country-southern food. The scent of candied yams and mac and cheese shot up my nose as I stuffed my phone into my pocket. While I wanted nothing more than to eat, drink some wine, and make love to Charlene all night, I had a lot on my mind. However, I wasn't sure if I should open up about this. I was embarrassed and afraid that she wouldn't understand. To ward off my anxiety, I spent the last few hours walking and watching videos until I couldn't anymore.

Exhausted, I tapped my keycard on the door fob, which pushed it open. Immediately, a whiff of dinner rushed over me, causing my mouth to water. The aroma full of love invited me in, facing Charlene, who stood wearing a short black lace robe with her hair flat to her head and as silky as could be. Her legs illuminated more than the last few nights. It was clear she had gotten a fresh wax.

Stressed, I threw my bookbag on the couch, creating a loud thud that even shocked me. Charla stumbled over with a puzzled look on her face. Tugging on my arm, her grip was comforting in itself.

"Babe, you alright?"

With my head hanging and defeat seeping into my soul, I growled, allowing the anger to fester. Charla immediately grabbed me by the arm and motioned me toward the suede couch in the suite's living area. The tenderness of her skin rubbing against my legs as she swung her feet back and forth put me in a more relaxed mood to actually open up to her. I didn't want to, but I needed to.

"Nah, I'm not."

"What's going on?" she inquired as she coaxed me, rubbing her soft, delicate hand along my wrist while sitting comfortably on my lap with her right arm around my neck.

I pulled my phone out of my pocket, unlocked it, and shuffled to Instagram. "See for yourself."

Charla grabbed the phone and adjusted the volume. Blaring through the speakers was carnival music and a sped-up version of me attacking Tati. My hands were wrung around her neck as anger filtered through my face. This video also featured the reaction from bystanders.

"Babe, what happened that caused this? Is that Tati?"

I nodded slowly. "Yes. That's Tati. She approached me in the library, yelling and out of control. Of course, she was mad that I hadn't been home for the last few days, but what really drove me over the edge was when she spoke about you and my mother."

"Me? What did she have to say about me?" Charla scrunched up her face, irritation on the brim of her lip.

"She said you're old enough to be my mother. Once she brought up my mother, I lost it!" My heart was beating, and my mind was turning as the words came out of my mouth. "I didn't mean to hurt her. I swear I didn't." I wiped back a lone tear from the side of my eye.

Charla fidgeted in my arms before raising her hand under my chin. Looking deeply into my eyes, she exhaled slowly.

"Baby, I'm so sorry she triggered you like that."

Her response threw me off. I didn't expect her to be this compassionate, especially after watching me choke the shit out of Tati. I don't know what I expected, but it was nice to know she wasn't pointing the finger at me. It felt like she was on my side.

"I feel like a bitch ass nigga for letting Tati trigger me. Now, because I lost my cool, I have to pay the consequences. I'm just hoping this doesn't affect me going to the NBA Draft."

"Have you spoken to your coach and got ahead of it? There has to be a way to spin this in your favor. Do you have a publicist?" Charla's eyes were soft, and her gaze was intentional and eager to help.

"No. I've been ignoring all calls from everyone. My coach called five times, and my team members have been texting me nonstop. I didn't know what to do. You were the first person I wanted to talk to," I admitted.

Locking eyes with Charla was intense, so I shifted my gaze to the cream-colored entertainment station where my Xbox sat. My eyes trailed from the antique champagne-tinted lamps on the end table to the cashmere carpet that covered the floors of the Four Seasons suite we'd shared for the last few days. Charla brought a homey vibe to the atmosphere despite the fact that I knew countless couples shared the same mattress that we first made love on. Just her essence turned this bleak suite into a homely abode.

"Look at me, baby, this is totally repairable. With the right publicist, you can spin this into a mental health campaign for Black men dealing with grief. Let me make some calls, and I'll get you out of this, baby. I just need you to trust me."

The sincerity in Charla's voice comforted me, putting my mind at ease.

"Are you sure? I've wanted to go to the NBA since I was a little boy. Just the thought that I jeopardized my chance is killing me."

Charla grabbed me by the tip of both ears, something my mother did to calm me down whenever I'd start panicking. "Baby, when I tell you I got you. I got you. I'm going to call my ex-husband's publicist. She's one of the best in sports management. Trust me, you're going to the NBA."

Charla said it with so much certainty that I was fetching every word out of her mouth like a cat licking the walls of his water bowl, hungry, savoring, and holding onto every crumb she gave me with dear life. She kept telling me to trust her as if she were bribing me, but the truth was that I trusted her more than anyone at the moment. Usually, my sister would be the first person I'd call after some shit like this, but I was more afraid to face Imani now than ever. She had a lot going on and had given so much of herself just to hold me and Dennis down. I couldn't disappoint her with this kind of news. Charlene wasn't just the woman I wanted to talk to. She was the only woman I needed to talk to. There was a time when Tati was the only woman I wanted advice from, but it was evident we were growing apart. Truthfully, I needed a woman, not a little ass girl, that would put me in a predicament to risk my entire fucking future.

I leaned forward and grabbed Charla's lips into mine. Our smiles melted into lust as we swirled tongues, swapping spit and groping each other. The heat between us intensified as I shimmied her succulent breasts out of the top of her robe and wrapped my lips around her areola. Her soft moans were so sexy, causing my dick to rise to attention. She snickered and rubbed her hand against my crotch, feeling for my shaft. I released her nipple from my mouth and began fondling her breasts, running the tips of my fingers against her nipples. She softly hissed, allowing me to take control of her body as we locked eyes. The next thing I knew, she unwrapped her robe, so I quickly pulled down my pants and slid in between her tight, gummy walls.

As Charla rode me, I felt every inch of her, my dick slapping against her canal like an uncontrollable water hose, ready to explode at any moment. She rocked and rocked, straddling me with her toned thighs and repeatedly thrusting her powerful pelvic onto my shaft to a melodic riddim. I enjoyed every moment of her pulsing pussy waterfall as her juices dripped onto my thighs.

As she rode and rode, I couldn't control myself. I released, shooting all my thick cream inside of her, completely unattached to the severity of the choice I had just made. In less than a week, I had broken up with Tati and gained a new woman and manager who I was all out raw dogging. While I was well aware that Charla and I just met, in the depths of my soul, I felt like I had known her my entire life. There was just something about our connection that I couldn't shake. All I knew was at this moment, I needed her.

gold digger

Imani

"ZION, BE NICE AND SHARE WITH YOUR GOD brother!" I roared, my tone a bit raspy and rude, but I was tired of repeating myself.

"No!" he blubbered, guarding the toy under his chest and hopping back so forcefully that he fell, hitting his tush on Crissy's newly installed hardwood floors. At four years old, Zion was growing into a little terror. His favorite word was no, and I was tired of hearing it.

My best friend Crissy was gracious in watching Zion for me two days a week and allowing him to run amuck in her home. She treated my baby like he was her own as we were family, and usually spent every other Sunday morning and afternoon together. This Sunday was no different. We just finished watching the church service, praying, worshipping, and nibbling on the homemade brunch

Crissy's husband, Jarvis, prepared. It didn't matter where Crissy moved to, her house was always homey, adorned with the best of Home goods décor, soft jasmine and vanilla fragrances, along with the latest and most modern upholstery. Most of all, Zion and I always felt welcomed.

"Come on, Ziony, be nice," Crissy begged in a soft, whiny voice. Zion eyed her suspiciously, tugging on his slobbery bottom lip before releasing the toy to her son Jalen and making his way into Crissy's lap.

I sucked my teeth, irritated that Zion had a difficult time following my instructions but would easily comply for Crissy, then melt right into puddy in her arms.

"I guess my voice isn't golden," I sassed, sitting up straight, pressing my spine into the back of the brown leather couch, and folding my arms.

"I just think it's the fact that I'm a teacher. My natural tone is rather more leveled and soothing," Crissy offered in a snooty-like, joking way as she snuggled my baby boy in her embrace.

Jalen, her son, six, was running in circles, most definitely burning his toes on the thick rug as he kicked and kicked, practicing his favorite karate moves and not paying us any attention whatsoever.

"Rather more, my ass!" I sassed back.

"See, that's your problem now — your potty mouth. Remind me exactly why I never let Jalen stay by you," Crissy joked.

"Oh, please. You know that's not the reason. The real reason is that you and Jarvis never do shit that requires a babysitter anyway with y'all boring asses."

Crissy shook her finger and sucked her teeth. "Don't bank on it for long, missy, 'cause Jarvis and Jalen just got their passports. Me and my boys are about to be out! Catch me while you can." Crissy giggled, then patted my leg softly. "And no, you're not welcomed."

"Damn, it's like that!" I screeched, my pitch high and exaggerated as I stood up from the couch and shuffled to the island protruding out of the kitchen.

"It's like that!" Crissy asserted, clicking her tongue against her teeth.

In the last few years, Crissy had transformed, losing forty pounds and taking her fitness journey seriously. She looked better than she had in high school, and there I was, twenty-five pounds overweight with a slight pudge that Rugga loved rubbing on, but I hated.

I grabbed another mimosa and stumbled back toward Crissy, pushing the champagne glass in her direction.

"Girl, you know two is my limit," Crissy declined as she looked away from me and started scrolling fiercely on her Android. Yes, Crissy switched to an Android two years ago, and it has made our routine morning FaceTime sessions nearly impossible. Now, we have to settle for WhatsApp's butchering service.

"You can ignore me all you want, bitch. I don't care. You gon' drink another one with me, the hell."

Lines deepened around Crissy's taut mouth as her eyes narrowed in on her screen. Dilated pupils and a furrowed brow painted her face as her mouth sat slightly agape.

"Is everything okay, girl?"

Crissy shook her head dramatically before removing

Zion from her lap and, getting up from the couch and forcing the phone in my face. "That's Darren, right?"

I snatched the phone from her hand and zeroed in on the shaky video of my brother choking a plus-size woman outside of one of USC's campus buildings. Determined to confirm my observations, I tapped the screen, and the video paused. Using my thumb and index finger, I zoomed in on the video. Inhaling deeply, I processed the visuals like data downloading into a computer and sighed. This was indeed Darren, and it was his girlfriend Tati, whom I had met only twice before. From the video, she looked bigger than I had last seen her, and the fact that she was half-naked also didn't help enhance her physique. She was a true BBW, with bountiful, full melons and a sizable tummy on a short five-foot-five frame.

"Yeah, that's him, alright!" I grouched almost a full two minutes later. "The NBA draft is in June. This is Darren's last shot to get into the league. Now is not the FUCKING time to be going viral for beating on women." I was furious.

First, I was disappointed as his sister, for I know Mommy and Daddy would be ashamed if they were alive. Even if Don were here, he would be disappointed to know Darren was abusing women. I tried not to think about the fact that I'd been guarding the secret for the last four years and that there was a strong possibility that Don was both Darren and Dennis' dad. Seeing as Don was dead, there was only one way of truly confirming if Don really was their dad, and that was conducting a DNA test between Dennis and Darren and one of Don's biological sons.

As much as I knew I'd have to tell them sooner or later,

it never seemed like the right time. Many times, I even questioned if telling them was necessary, especially considering that it was possible Don was the father, while also a strong possibility that he wasn't. Why rock the boat just for it not to be true?

"Damn. It's not looking good for Dice. You need to call him," Crissy asserted.

Scrolling through the comments, nothing but hateful, vile words were spewed on the post.

"Men with mommy issues always beating on women. Didn't his mother commit suicide?" one user wrote.

"That's his NBA career right down the drain. How sad! I can't say I'm surprised at his carelessness. Athletes are stupid," another user wrote.

Anger began festering in my heart as I inhaled and exhaled, my wrists rattling with tension. Frustrated, I quickly dialed Darren's number and scurried out Crissy's sliding door. The phone rang several times before going to voicemail. I redialed it, but this time, it only rang twice before the voicemail greeting appeared again.

"Answer the phone, Darren!" I screeched aloud, my scattered voice vibrating through my chest.

Knowing Darren, he was completely zoned out and would likely ignore my calls for days. Considering the seriousness of the situation, I knew Darren needed his sister by his side, and he expected me to show up whether or not he said it. I opened and shut my eyes several times, rolling over thoughts in my mind. I pinched my lips together once. My mind was made up. I eagerly stepped back into the house, met by Crissy's bewildered facial expression.

"I'm going to LA. Darren needs me."

I DIDN'T TAKE any real time to think or contemplate my next move. Within an hour, I booked three flights, one for myself, Zion, and Rugga. Usually, I would leave Zion with Crissy, but I felt a strong urge to be with my baby, especially since this was a family-related trip, so it was only right that I had Zion with me. Despite how fussy Zion could be, looking in his eyes whenever difficulties arose always put me at ease. His light hazel pubs reminded me of his father. In fact, the bigger Zion got, the more he resembled his Uncle Darren, which explained how close they were. I knew Darren would be happy to see his nephew, and now, more than ever, he needed to be surrounded by love.

In times like this, I wish Don were here. Since he was a former pro athlete who battled many scandals throughout his career, he'd know exactly what to do and who to contact. Unfortunately, all I knew to do was call my publicist, who didn't specialize in the sports arena at all. Nonetheless, she connected me with the top sports publicist in LA whom Darren and I had a scheduled meeting with as soon as I touched down.

Our flight was set to take off in three hours, and Darren still wasn't answering the phone. Not until I texted him in all caps, stating that I was flying into LA later that day, did it make him respond.

Darren: *Cool. Meet me at this address: 8899 Beverly Blvd.*

Relieved, Rugga and I boarded the plane with my baby boy in tow. After I settled into my seat and situated Zion with his squishy pillow behind his head, Dennis ran through my mind. Growing up, Dennis and Darren had been thick as thieves, but as soon as Momma and Daddy passed, Dennis distanced himself from all of us. He began dabbling in drugs and hanging out with the wrong crowd. Now, he was so far gone that having a logical conversation with him, especially about something so important, was nearly impossible. Second, being out in public with him was so unpredictable that I couldn't take a chance at humiliating Darren even more, so as much as I would have loved for my brother to be here, having Dennis around just wasn't a good idea.

"You good, baby?" Rugga purred into my ear as he snuggled me into a one-armed embrace.

As I rested my head on him, his hot breath slapped across my neck, causing the hairs on my skin to rise. Now chewing on my earlobe, my head was pressed against the window as Rugga soothed me to sleep.

"Yeah, baby, I'm good."

WE HAD JUST LANDED by the time I woke up from my nap. Pulling into our terminal, the aircraft stopped, and the clink clacks from passengers releasing their seat belts belted through the plane. I watched as Rugga got Zion together, helping him put on his shoes, jacket, and backpack. Rugga was so good with Zion, which made it easy for me to love him because he loved a part of me that was so sacred — my seed.

With a twinkle in my eye, I bit my lips as I thought about how good I was gon' lay it on Rugga once we settled in. After taking a virtual tour of the condo Darren was renting, I was tempted to cancel my reservations at the Four Seasons. He had more than enough room to accommodate us at this new place that I knew nothing of. Something was definitely going on with Darren. Between the fight with Tati, moving to a new place without telling me, and not answering my calls, I didn't know what my baby brother was going through, but I was determined to find out.

We rode in the Mercedes Benz rental to Darren's place in complete silence. Even Zion was quiet, which was rare for his chatty self. After we parked in the parking lot, we exited the vehicle on a standard city-looking block. I looked up at the modernized high rise building in front of us. This was prime real estate for sure in the heart of West Beverly Hills. *Expensive.*

I wonder if he was renting or if he made the leap and actually bought a piece of real estate without my and Rugga's help. *Hmm.*

We tiptoed inside toward the elevators, bypassing security and not fully taking in the sleek, high-tech décor. I was in front and Rugga and Zion were a few steps behind me with our luggage. My eyes squinted, getting smaller and smaller as I tried to process what I was seeing. As my vision became clearer, I folded my arms and inhaled through my nose. My heart was beating, my blood was boiling, and I could feel how tight my facial muscles had stiffened.

"What the fuck are you doing here, Charlene?" I bucked in full defense mode. Rugga was now beside me, with an even more aggressive stance.

"Zion, sit down," Rugga instructed my baby to sit on the small chaise in the corner. Zion did as he was told without backtalk or exaggeration, which was his usual response whenever Rugga told him to do something.

"Is everything alright, baby?" he interjected, breaking the awkwardness between Charlene and me.

"Nah, I'm trying to figure out what the fuck this bitch is doing at my brother's apartment?"

A smile danced on Charlene's face as she chuckled and released her folded arms. She was wearing a cotton white cami with gray skin-tight boxer briefs that cupped her ass perfectly and white thong slippers boasting four stacked diamond anklets on her right leg. Extending her arm, she reached for Rugga's hand and shook it forcefully.

"My name is Charlene, and I'm a friend to the family. Imani and I haven't always seen eye to eye, but I'm hoping we can get past it, especially considering that I'll be around more."

Rugga eyed her up and down before snatching his hand back. Years had passed since I last saw Charlene, but nothing had changed with her. She was still as scandalous as ever. For one, how she was dressed was completely inappropriate to be prancing around an apartment building, especially shaking my man's hand. I was so happy Rugga was a militant ass nigga who wasn't thirsty or impressed by an old bitch with a BBL.

"The fuck you mean you'll be around more?"

Charlene licked her lips seductively and laughed. "Ask your brother. He'll tell you."

Nostrils flaring, I still managed to clear my throat, which created a nasty, repulsive sound that represented exactly how I felt about Charlene.

"Bitch, you're so fucking lucky that I've healed, and I'm a lady now. Otherwise, I would drag your fucking ass all throughout this building."

"And you're lucky that I'm a grown ass woman with a whole lot of class to simply dismiss your ratchet commentary. Really, it's out of love and respect for your brother that I won't gather your ass up right now. And it's the respect I have for your man that I won't air your dirty laundry right out in front of him. But if you try me, who knows? I'd advise you to slow your fucking roll, little girl."

Shit was beginning to get real nasty, and before I embarrassed myself in front of my man, I stormed off, stepping into the elevator. Charlene, Zion, and Rugga followed behind me, and the time it took to get to the fifth floor felt like an eternity. My eyes were burning a hole into Charlene's neck as I stood behind her, wanting to knock her fucking head into the wall. I closed my eyes for a moment, not wanting to exchange glances with Rugga anymore. I knew he was watching my every move, and I knew he had questions I didn't want to answer.

As we got off the elevator, visions of kicking Charlene straight into her back and pouncing on her ass fluttered through my mind several times. Leading the way, knowing that my man and I were behind her, she switched even harder as she put each foot directly in front of another, causing her hips to sway back and forth. I sucked my teeth loudly, and at this point, I didn't give a fuck. I simply wanted to know what the fuck was going on between her and Darren.

When we approached the door, I stepped in front of Charlene, side-mushing her. Knocking on the door wildly, I stood with my hands on my hips, waiting for Darren to open the fucking door.

"Babe, why you ain't use the keycard," he said before looking up and noticing me.

"Babe? You fucking this old gold digger?" I wailed, pushing my way past him into the apartment.

Inside, it was immaculate, high-tech, and sleek but with a sophisticated aura, adorned with soft accents like the abstract-shaped lamp on the end table near the stairs. The aroma also screamed mature, and I just knew Charlene's ass had to be behind it.

"Yo, Mani, watch your mouth talking about my lady," Darren checked me.

I turned around, eyes wild and truly confused. "Your lady? You can't be fucking serious. You do know this is Don's ex-wife, right? You know she hated Momma, and a few months before Momma died, I had to fuck her up for talking about Momma. And on top of that, she's older than Momma." I yelled!

"And? You were fucking your own godfather who is thirty years older than you. You have no room to judge!" Darren spat out.

At this point, Rugga had grabbed Zion up and disappeared out of sight. I was grateful that he gave us some privacy and was hoping that Charlene would follow suit and allow me and my brother to talk alone, but of course, her heathen ass didn't. She stood beside Darren like we were all having an open conversation. I may have spoken openly to the room, but she knew damn well I wasn't addressing her. I didn't care how many years it had been. Charlene and I would never be cool, and that was a guarantee.

"Look, Darren, this is different. What Don and I had was natural. We were in love. Can't you see that this old cougar bitch is a gold digger, and her getting with you is purely money motivated? Don took care of me. He left me one hundred million dollars. This bitch is broke. She can't take care of you. She still living off alimony," I raged.

"Ain't nothing over here broke, baby. I've been handling mine for a long time. Unlike you, I'm a grown ass woman, and I don't need a man to take care of me," Charlene hissed, waving her finger in my face.

"I'm gon' need you to back the fuck up before shit gets critical in here. Darren, get your hoe!"

Darren, whose face was slack and emotionless, stepped in the middle of us and dragged me away.

"Mani, I know you probably came down here because

you were concerned about the video circulating, and I appreciate your care, but you can't come into my home with my lady and start all this commotion. I'm going through too much to settle a fight between two women I love."

"Love? How long have you been fucking this bitch?"

"Imani, she's not a bitch. You know her fucking name, so show some fucking respect. It hasn't been long, but we're together, and that's all that matters."

I stared my brother up and down in disgust, my lip scrunched, and mouth pouted. "You tender dick little nigga. She must be putting the works on you. Well, you better hope she's good for more than sucking and fucking and can get you out of this bullshit mess you got yourself in."

"Actually, she's got it all sorted out. I've already met with my PR rep, and we have a closed press conference tomorrow. You're actually not needed, but thanks for coming all this way, sis. Appreciate it," Darren sarcastically remarked before leaning over, pecking me on the cheek, and yanking me by the wrist toward the door. I couldn't believe my little brother was putting me out in front of this bitch.

"RUGGA! LET'S GO!" I yelled out as I saw that Darren was ready to close the door on my face. As I peered into the door, Charlene was standing on the stairs so I could get a good view of her. Folding her arms, she had a sly smirk sitting on the brim of her mouth, making me want to knock the amusement off her face.

"RUGGA!" I barked for the second time. He quickly

appeared with a look of confusion on his face and Zion in tow. "Come on. We're out of here!"

Rugga scooted by Darren, looking him up and down before we walked off, both stunned. Now, we were in LA for a week with no agenda, yet I had a lot of explaining to do for my man to understand what the fuck was truly going on.

big dick energy

Charlene

"I don't give a fuck about you being Don's ex-wife, but when exactly were you going to tell me that you and my moms had beef?" Darren roared, his eyes brood yet wild as he intently stared at me.

Despite the uneasiness in his tone, I couldn't help ogling over him and how well he cleaned up. Dressed in a navy blue five-piece suit with shiny gold cufflinks blinging off his wrists, Darren looked at least thirty as he stood, right leg across the other, against the elevator on the floor of our condo building. As much as I didn't want to argue with him, there was no way I could avoid it. What made it more difficult was that I knew truthfully answering his question would hurt his feelings.

"Babe, let's talk about this after the press conference.

My only focus right now is that you impress these people, portray a cool demeanor, and improve your image."

Darren cleared his throat and inhaled deeply through his nostrils. "Nah, we're addressing this shit right here and right the fuck now! You had smoke for my moms?" The muscles in his face tightened, his jaw stiffened, and his brows were crunched together.

Anger was sexy on him. To be honest, how he stood up for his momma was sexy to me. I was just curious as to why he waited until we got outside the apartment to address me. When I thought about how quiet he was and the fact that he spent most of yesterday in the gym, it made sense that he was reacting late. Clearly, he needed time to process all that happened, and for that, I respected it. Either way, it was turning me on.

Lightheartedly, I giggled, stepping closer and closer to him until his back and my hand both touched the wall. Invading all of his personal space, I simpered. "Of course not. Bonita and I had our differences, but I wouldn't call it beef. It was more like misunderstandings and a difference of opinions... on many things." I bit my lip and inhaled. "Still, I respected your mother as a mother and a woman. She did a great job with you."

I was laying it on thick at this point, but there was a method to my madness. I didn't feel comfortable calling his mother a hoe to his face. I'm not sure how much he knew about Bonita and Don's relationship, but I wasn't taking on the burden of revealing that information. I was only concerned about our relationship and what it meant for my future, and if that meant protecting Darren's peace by withholding information, then so be it. In fact, since Imani was so fucking grown, she was going to have to tell her brother the truth about their mother. That wasn't my responsibility.

"Oh, okay. That's exactly what I thought. I knew Imani's ass was lying. It seems like you and Imani have issues over fucking the same nigga," he crassly blurted out.

"You mean my husband? It could never be beef over what was mine and what was never hers. That is... legally."

Darren sucked his teeth. "Oh, please. Imani may not have been his wife, but she got more money than you from his estate, and I know that for a fact."

Darren's mouth was slick, and that reality stung me like an annoying bloodsucking bee. Pulling away from him, I stepped back, rubbing my hands from my elbows up my arms. "That's what happens when you're under thirty, with perky titties and no kids and an uber-tight pussy," I remarked.

Nervously, I pressed the button for the elevator, anxious to move out of this awkward, insecure space I was standing in. I was officially the old bitch. When it came to Bonita, I couldn't compete because she had Don's heart, and when it came to Imani, I was just the old haggard widow. It seemed like I was constantly battling a Bleeker woman. Bonita and I bumped heads for years, especially once I figured out that she was Don's main side bitch. While he fucked other women, Bonita was the one who had his heart. Out of respect for Don and Rob's friendship, I never caused any waves or mentioned anything to Rob. I hid their secret for years like it was mine. I couldn't break an innocent man's heart, and just like his daddy, Darren is an innocent party in this matter, too.

"Look, Charlene. I like older women. Even my ex-girlfriend Tati is older. Therefore, I don't need you getting all insecure on me. These young bitches ain't got shit on you, and you know that."

The elevator came, and Darren guided me by the arm inside, holding me carefully and with a keen sense of certainty. It was weird, but he made me feel exactly how Don had — protected.

"Confidence! That's one of the main reasons I love older women. There is no need to overcompensate. Just be sexy and certain of one's self. I need you to walk in that at all times!" Darren commanded. Here he was, younger than my sons, knocking the Mario coins out of my pussy and attempting to give me a lecture on self-esteem.

Life truly humbles you as you age.

I giggled to myself, realizing that my insecurities had turned into admiration as my eyes glistened while looking at Darren, stunned and in awe. Now, in the elevator, the closeness of the walls and the dimness of the lights brought a flair of intimacy that danced between us. It still amazed me how much big dick/ big dog energy this young ass man had.

Meekly, I lowered my head and bunched my lips together. "Okay, baby," I cooed.

I knew that a big part of our connection was me making him feel good, but little did he know he made my old ass feel young and alive again. I was impressed with the excitement, the sex, his swag, and how he handled me and situations. Even in how he went with the flow and quickly pivoted and adapted, from leaving his girlfriend the first day he met me to standing up to Imani and, most of all, taking accountability for the viral video.

As we got off the elevator and made our way through the lobby, hand in hand, an awkwardly tall and super thin white woman, who resembled an older version of Paris Hilton, met us.

"Darren Bleeker. Susan Talari, I'm a senior publicist from Creative Arts Agency. Nice to meet you."

Darren hesitated but slowly raised his hand to hers, and they exchanged handshakes.

"Charlene Moore Davidson. Nice to meet you," I introduced myself, leaning forward and exchanging side pecks. "So what's the plan?" I didn't fail to jump right into it.

Balancing her iPad in one arm, she dabbed her stylus pen along the screen as her eyes fluttered rapidly. " Uhh, the plan is accountability and mental health, as we discussed before. Darren, did you work on the speech I emailed you?"

Exhaling, Darren nodded. "Yeah, I got it down pact."

"GOOD AFTERNOON, everyone. My name is Susan Talari, and I am a senior publicist with Creative Arts Agency, representing Darren 'Dice' Bleeker. On behalf of my client, with a truly humbled and apologetic heart. From the mouth of Dice himself, he wants to open with a statement."

I tried my best not to stare too hard at any of the fawn-colored white men in front of me. All seven of them were old, at least in their seventies. I squinted my eyes as I caught a glimpse of the one redhead across from me, breathing rapidly, mimicking an overly excited pig. I turned my head to Darren, who stood up from his seat.

"Hello, gentlemen. First, I'd like to start by saying that my time at USC and serving the Trojans has been a phenomenal experience and one that I would never take for granted. While it may not seem like that due to the nature of the viral video we are here to discuss, I'll have you know I take full accountability for my actions, and I terribly regret the choices I have made. Not to make an excuse, but I'd like to walk you through my time at USC to provide clarity and understanding." Darren announced, finally taking a pause.

He scanned the faces of each man he presented his case to and resumed speaking.

"I came to USC as a freshman after losing my mother to suicide and my father to MS. I managed to get all As and Bs throughout my tenure as a student, serve as the president of the student council for two years in a role where I led USC to do the most community service in the entire country all while battling depression, loneliness, and immense stress as a student and star athlete." Darren's voice started to crack a bit as he paused again, this time inhaling so deeply his chest began heaving.

Rubbing my hands together, they were sweaty as I was nervous for my baby. Although he made it look easy with how he was handling this level of accountability, I knew it was tearing him up inside to get this vulnerable, especially in front of all these crackers. I was relieved I could be by his side as we were the only two Black people in a room of twelve individuals. Even the transcriber, their lawyer, and the head of security were white. As I tapped my fingernails against the table, I pondered on the fact that there were even so many unnecessary people in this session. Why did we need security for a private meeting? A silent racial microaggression I took heed to as I sighed and shook my head.

"The video that is circulating campus is due to pent-up grief and a lack of safe spaces for Black male students to work through their emotions. My family, especially my younger brother and I both, have been struggling with mental health issues since the passing of our parents. In fact, my brother has been diagnosed with bipolar depression and has been deteriorating ever since."

Darren's neck lowered as he swallowed his bottom lip. Forcing his hands into his pockets, he scanned the entire room before resuming.

"As far as me, I've used basketball, studying, and partying as an escape because those are the only outlets that USC provides for students who look like me. The three times I pursued therapy at the student mental health clinic, I was always told that there was a long waiting list and to sign up and wait for a callback that never came. Again, I am not making excuses or blaming USC. I am simply stating that if the opportunity to finish my last basketball season and or graduate is taken away from me, I don't know how I'll manage as playing basketball here at USC is my life, my therapy, and provides me with mental discipline to manage. With the help of USC and my publicist, I am hoping to get the mental health resources that I need to cope with the grief I've been experiencing."

Darren bowed his head and sat down. Susan hopped up from her seat, rubbed her hands together, interlocked them, and nodded her head.

"As you can see, gentlemen, my client takes full accountability for his actions and wants to reconcile so long as no disciplinary action is upheld. Rather, my client is willing to make a public statement of accountability, attend anger management therapy, and even become the face of Black male mental health at USC. In fact, a new order of business I'd like to propose is a collaboration with Black Men Cry, the nation's largest mental health organization for Black men. I already have an endorsement deal on the table that is most definitely beneficial and of monetary gain for USC."

Eyeing the faces of all seven men on the committee, I searched for clues of validation, disdain and/or approval. After glancing back and forth, I was stuck between seven different poker faces. If it was one thing white folks were good at, it was hiding their wicked intentions. White folks knew to maintain a poker face to retain power and strength, and these motherfuckers had a field day with it today.

The man in the fourth seat cleared his throat and sat up in his seat with pinched, thin lips. Placing his arms on the table, he scrunched up his nose. As I looked closer, two red cold sores sat in plain sight atop his lip as he opened his mouth to talk. I immediately closed my mouth to swallow the engrossed embarrassment. *Disgusting.*

"While we, the university, are in support of Darren Bleeker remaining on the team and graduating, we cannot stop the victim from pressing charges and or censoring the speech of any student organizations or larger organizations outside of the university from speaking out against you. USC will not provide that kind of protection. USC also cannot combat with scouters or the NBA on your behalf. We are not in the business of reputation management for any students, MVP or not. Brand reputation, as you know, Ms. Talari is the responsibility of an outside representative. Now, as far as promoting Black male mental health as a campaign campus-wide, we believe it is a great idea, but to roll it out now at such a vulnerable time is not ideal. Perhaps in a year or two after you've graduated, we can circle back to that in our university planning. As of now, our practice is to take accountability and then let things die down. I'd suggest you bring your A-game this last season. In my experience, nothing saves a reputation better than winning a championship. Keep your head in the game, son, and you'll be okay!"

He spit that shit out like he recited it at least fifty times. Although a lengthy monologue, his diction was fluid, with no hiccups, interruptions, or even an inflection of compassion riddled in his throat. Sharp, callous, and uncaring, it was obvious that they didn't give a fuck about Darren, and their only concern was USC.

Susan raised her hand in refute before swallowing hard. "Thank you, gentlemen, so much for your time, grace, and accommodations. While we respect the decision USC has made to not help in the fight to bring awareness to the importance of mental health resources for Black men on this very campus at this time, we'd like to inform you that Darren will still move forward with the Black Men Cry endorsement. Due to your close association with Darren, we believe it's only right that you are aware of how his likeness will be used." Susan bowed her head, showing respect to her white counterparts before tucking her lips closed. "If there isn't anything left to discuss, to my understanding, Darren will be attending basketball practice tomorrow, as usual."

The room was gripping with unsettled, silent tension masked by professionalism and separated by an oversized black office table. The shortest and oldest white man who sat the farthest to the right interjected. Struggling to stand, he finally did, his small hand leaning onto the edge of the table.

"Darren won't return to practice..." his throat croaked, the dryness producing a nasally sound, "until after he publicly takes accountability and hosts a successful campus-wide town hall." He paused, his chest heaving before cracking a whimsical smile. "Which can be scheduled for as early as the next few weeks."

Susan, Dice, and I all looked at each other, panic wretched over all of our faces.

"I'm sorry, sir, but one of the biggest games in my career is next week. We were hoping we could host the town hall this week." Darren was sitting perfectly straight up and erect in his seat, his head protruding forward.

The white men all looked down the table to the last seat, where all the power was apparently held. The oldest man, who had just finished speaking, nodded his head, silver patches visible all over his scalp.

"The earliest we are willing to do for a press conference is next Monday. However, you still are prohibited from attending practice."

Darren shook his head several times. "But the game is on Thursday. I need enough time to practice. I've already missed a few days."

A huff rolled out of his mouth. "Well, make sure you stay in touch with Coach George for all workout routines so you can practice solo until you return to practice with the team on Tuesday. The Office of the President will have its assistant reach out to you with details for the town hall." Gritting his teeth, he snickered. "This meeting is over. Enjoy the rest of your day, everyone," he dismissively concluded before the group gathered themselves and simmered out of the office, leaving me, Darren, and Susan sitting there puzzled.

confrontation

Dice

"I THOUGHT YOU DIDN'T HAVE THAT NIGGA'S LAST name anymore?" I questioned, truly perplexed, why she introduced herself as Charlene Moore Davidson to my publicist. After that annoying ass meeting and having to track down Coach George all day, we were finally back in the condo, standing in the living room.

Comfortable in her robe and fuzzy slippers, Charlene's eyes lowered in submission as her cheeks puffed out.

"You ain't think I forgot that shit did you?"

Charlene rapidly shook her head until a smile appeared on her lips. "Aww, look at you all jealous and shit." She chuckled, leaning forward and pinching both sides of my cheeks.

I brushed her off before folding my arms. "Stop fucking playing with me."

Huffing and puffing, Charlene sighed. Rolling her eyes, she licked her lips and tilted her head. "Baby, relax! It's not like that. Names and associations help build reputation and respect." With hands moving in vivid motion, she continued, "Your publicist is some boujie white bitch at the top sports agency in the world. I am the ex-wife of a global heavyweight champion. Of course, I was going to use my leverage to benefit you."

My suspicious gaze instantly turned into a warm simper. *This bitch always knows what to say.*

"I guess that makes sense," I responded, my aggression trailing off. Just when I started to relax, anxiety perked up, causing anger to reappear. I stepped back, taking a full look at Charla with mere distrust in my chest.

"There are two kinds of bitches in this world that I dislike, a sneaky bitch and a devious bitch. And withholding the fact that you not only knew me and my whole family, but that you were connected to me and MY WHOLE FAMILY was some devious ass shit. And that kind of shit will get your ass cut the fuck off." My chest was heaving as I watched Charlene's face go slack. "However, because you've been holding a nigga down throughout this entire bullshit, I'ma give yo' ass a pass and let this shit slide, this ONE TIME."

A weight felt like it had rolled off my shoulder simply by expressing myself. I had been carrying that shit all day, along with the fact that I had to face the university and the world as an angry, sad, mad Black man, and as if things couldn't get worse, I was restricted from practicing with the team the entire week before the biggest game of my career.

Shit wasn't looking good at such a critical time, and I didn't know what to do. Shit with Imani and I had gone left quick, and Tati and I were done. Charlene was all I had at the moment, and the thought of her deceiving me didn't sit well with me.

Charlene's lips were puckered as she swayed forward. Pulling my hand into hers, she guided me to the white leather couch and sat me down. In an instant, she was saddled in my lap with the sincerest eyes and softest lips.

"The last thing I want is for you to distrust me." Pinching her lips together, she ran her hand over my head, massaging my three-sixty waves. Her touch brought healing to my body, but I was still angry inside.

"So don't lie to me or hide shit from me!" I bucked defensively.

Charlene wiggled her hips deeper into my lap as she gripped my chin and stroked it with her thumb, "Okay, baby. From here on out, no more withholding information. I'm going to be open, honest, and transparent. Mark my words."

Taking a deep breath, Charla looked me into my eyes with a spirit so familiar and angelic, something I had never seen in another woman other than my Momma, and she rubbed on the bottom half of my earlobe. Her touch was endearing and comforting. Her scent was as soothing as her golden skin, simply irresistible.

"Look, babe, here's the truth. I was already all in when I found out you were Bonita and Rob's boy. You had already captivated me. For you to be so young, so charming, so disciplined, and so damn smart blew me away." Charlene's cheeks were deep pink, not quite red, but it was obvious that she was blushing. "I didn't want to rob us of the opportunity of love, lust, or whatever the fuck we've got going on here. I didn't want bad blood that neither one of us caused to be the reason we couldn't be."

Hearing her talk like this solidified it for me. We were both falling for each other, and the fact that it was happening so fast and didn't scare either of us was dangerous in itself. We didn't give a fuck.

"I'm happy you didn't allow you and Imani's drama to get between me and you..."

Before I could finish my statement, Charlene put her index finger to my lips, hushing me.

"Baby, if I'm going to be transparent, I must stop you there. The beef has never been between your sister and me. It always started with Bonita because before Imani started fucking my ex-husband, your mother and Don were involved in an affair for years."

The sun cast a shadow through the apartment, hitting the rug and the wall beside it as darkness invaded my eyes. I flinched forward, almost dropping Charlene from my lap, but her holding onto my shirt prevented her from falling.

"My mother wasn't fucking Don. You must be out of yo' ' rabbit ass mind, lady."

To instantly go from loving Charlene to hating her fucking guts was truly magic, but when it came to my momma, I'd go to war with anybody.

Charlene stumbled off me, now folding her arms with her hips to the side. "Darren, I know this shit doesn't sound good, but it's the real gritty truth. And frankly, I never wanted to be the one to tell you. I wanted to leave it to Imani because I never felt like it was my place to." Charlene's shoulders raised before she rubbed her hands together. "But you told me not to lie to you and not to hide shit from you. And if we gon' be together, the lies and innuendos stop now. You asked for the truth, but the question is, can you handle it?"

With a scrunchy nose and fire in my eyes, I exhaled deeply. Getting up from the couch, Charlene and I never broke eye contact. Balling up my hands, I felt the aggression building. I felt the tears forming in my eyes.

No wonder Imani and Momma were going through it after Imani moved in with Don. They, too, were fighting over the same nigga. Meanwhile, both were too damn occupied to look out for Daddy when he was diagnosed with MS. My father died because of them. My mind was so warped from all the thoughts I was processing and everything I was putting together that I didn't know what to think. All I knew was that my hatred for Imani was strengthening.

"Babe, are you okay?" Charlene asked, breaking me out of my thoughts.

"NO. This shit doesn't sit right with me. My parents have been gone for five years, and I'm finally getting clarity as to what happened to them. I never believed that my momma would take her own life, and the fact that she did it at Don's home never made sense to me. Still, it's all coming together now. Don killed my momma, and Imani knew it and kept it from me all this time."

Charlene loudly gulped as she shook her head rapidly.

"No, Darren. Don was deeply in love with your mother. He loved her in ways he never loved me. If I had to guess, I would say that he was only with Imani to spite your mother because Bonita was the love of his life. There's no way he could have killed her."

I bit my lip and inhaled deeply. I was so conflicted. A huge part of me believed every word Charlene said. Sincerity based her lips, and there was no way she was lying. Yet another part of me still was skeptical that foul play had occurred. And maybe not from Don, but Imani had something to do with this shit.

Did my sister really kill our mother over a piece of dick? Over an old ass man who was her godfather? I didn't know what the fuck had happened, but I was going to find Imani and get to the bottom of this shit.

sibling rivalry

Imani

SEVERE LOUD POUNDS BOUNCED OFF THE WALLS OF the hotel suite that Rugga and I had been staying in for the last few days. Although I couldn't get a hold of Darren, Rugga and I decided to stay in LA for a week and enjoy the mini vacation we never got to take. Out of it from the last three sessions of lovemaking we had, I rolled over Rugga, who was softly snoring and stepped into my favorite travel slippers. Made of memory foam, they supported my feet lovely. Before walking past Zion's room, I peeked inside and found him sleeping wildly. I chuckled to myself. That boy was a sleeping warrior, fighting whatever demons were in his nightmares. The pounding persisted again and again, causing me to close Zion's room door.

Who the fuck was this banging this loud on our door? I glanced at my Apple watch and saw it was a quarter after seven p.m. The sun had disappeared, and it was dark out from the looks of the indigo-blue sky boasting through the windows. In front of the door, I stood on my tippy toes to look through the peephole when the pounding continued, now vibrating against my cheek.

My eyebrows rose, and my mouth began twitching when I saw it was Darren. *What the fuck did he want?*

I opened the door quickly and found him alone, without Charlene, which I was grateful for. However, his energy was on ten as he stood there with a deep, penetrating scowl.

"So, you ignore my calls for days and show up to my hotel suite unannounced? How did you even know where we were?"

Shoving his way inside, even bumping me on the shoulder, Darren scoffed. "Worrying about how I found where you were staying should be the least of your worries. And I only showed up here to get answers! So I'm the only one who's asking the fucking questions here! Do you understand me?"

The veins on the side of Darren's temple protruded from his head. I had never seen my brother this irate. I backed up slowly as I carefully watched him. Unsure of exactly what he was capable of and what answers he wanted, my nerves were running wild.

"Did you know that Momma had been having an affair with Don for years?"

The question took me by surprise. I wasn't quite prepared to answer this, especially considering I had deeply buried it these past few years. I hated thinking about the fact that my momma had a long history with Don, who was not only my lover but also the father of my son. Although I missed my momma terribly, it was a relief not having her here. I got to pretend that Don and I had the perfect love story and that he just tragically died. I didn't have to think about the truth. I held the truth in my heart for so long because I was scared to release the pain. Having to face Darren wasn't easy.

I shook my head slowly. "Yes."

"How long did their affair go on, and how long did you know?"

I exhaled deeply. That's when shit became muddy. I, myself, didn't have all the answers.

"Darren, I was a kid during most of this, and you weren't even born. I hadn't learned they were together until Don and I were already in too deep. I was already in love with him." I simpered as love and war clogged up my throat.

As much as I loved Don, being with him created a war between my mother and me, and I wish I could get the time back. I wish I could get to spend another day with her. I'd give it all up, even my baby Zion, just to talk to my momma again.

Darren's chin was stiff, and his nostrils flared. "Imani, do you hear yourself? You were a little girl. That old ass man took advantage of you just to spite Momma. Don't you see that?"

His words were the dart, and my heart was on the board. He hit me right in the bullseye with that comment. It hurt so badly that I instantly felt queasy.

"It wasn't like that with Don and me," I muttered.

"It was exactly like that. You just don't wanna admit it. You were nothing more than a piece of young pussy to Don. According to Charlene, his heart was always with Momma."

I leaned over as my stomach turned in defeat. I felt sick from Darren's words. Don was the love of my life. Hearing from my own brother that I was just a piece of pussy to the man I procreated with, to the man who killed my rapist, who took care of me while he was here and even while he's gone made me feel some type of way.

With tears streaming down my face, I leaped forward and slapped the shit out of Darren. His face turned fiery red as he stood there without even flinching.

"You're lucky as fuck that I got too much respect for you and Momma because if you were a bitch on the street, I would have two-pieced your fucking ass. But as we both know, I don't need any more negative press from beating another stupid hoe's ass, so I'ma let you have it, but I need you to answer one more question for me."

I backed up from my brother, moving toward the living room but never keeping my eyes off him. His letting me slide with that slap had me on edge, fearful that he'd pounce on me at any moment. Holding my hands up as I continued to back up, I nodded. "What?"

"Did Daddy know she was cheating with Don?"

I slowly nodded as I watched his world shatter.

"Momma broke him. She killed Daddy slowly with heartbreak. All those years, she was fucking his best friend and still playing house as the perfect wife and mother.

Meanwhile, she was a hoe, just like you! What kind of bitch fucks behind her mother?"

Anger was festering in my soul. I couldn't believe him.

"There you go, judging me when you have no idea what love even is. You don't know what it's like to be with someone who believes in you, makes your dreams come true or being with someone who protects you. All you know how to do is fuck fat broke bitches and old, washed-up widows that you have to take care of with my money. You can't speak on shit I did because you ain't ever had what I had."

I was livid. This motherfucker thought he was better than me when he was fucking behind his daddy. The only difference was that, unlike me, he didn't even know who his biological father was. I used to feel obligated to tell the boys who their daddy was, and I swore that one of these days, I would. Still, truthfully, with the way Darren was talking to me, I wasn't telling him a damn thing. From now on, he was on my shit list. The nigga could die without knowing who his father was for all I cared. I refused to tolerate disrespect from a motherfucker I raised from the time I was twelve.

"Is everything alright in here?"

I turned around and saw a groggy Rugga. Sleep was riddled all in his throat.

"Yeah, babe. Everything good, Darren was just leaving."

Rugga's brows bunched together. "But you've been trying to get a hold of him for days. If you guys need some privacy, I'll take Zion out for food and leave you two to talk. Just let me know, babe."

"Nah, babe. It's no need for that. As I said, Darren was just leaving." My voice was a bit elevated as I turned my back on Rugga, now facing Darren, whose lip was twisted, and eyes were turned up.

"It's all good, my man. I was just leaving," Darren reiterated. As he opened the door to exit, he turned back around. "Don't make the same mistake my father did by marrying a slut, my man. It killed him. I don't want the same to happen to you."

"IMANI, talk to me. What the fuck is going on between you and Darren?" Rugga inquired as he stood with his arms folded, his gaze intense while looking at me with bewildered eyes. "It took everything in me not to knock his little ass out for talking out the side of his neck. You saved his ass, forreal, ma. He's one lucky little nigga."

I loved it when Rugga showed how overprotective he was of me. It was so sexy. It turned me on to see my man ready to go to war about me, even against my brother. Standing in the bathroom with his shirt off, exposing his washboard abs, strong arms, and muscles, I licked my lips at the sight before me. It never got old looking at his chocolate skin radiating under the light.

"Don't worry about it, babe. Darren's just feeling himself. He's got a piece of that cougar pussy and done lost his motherfucking mind." I exhaled a long breath before wrapping my arms around him.

Pulling him into me, I latched onto him, my legs now

wrapped around his as I puckered my lips out for a kiss. Rugga plopped his hands under my butt as he held me up, my body suspended around him. We passionately kissed as he wobbled toward the bed.

"You better get your brother in check because next time he comes out his face to my woman, it's gon' be me and him, and it ain't nothing you can do to stop it," Rugga asserted, his lip rode up in aggression as a snarl permeated his mouth.

I bit my lip and exhaled. "I love when you get like this. You don't play about your bitch."

Rugga sucked his teeth and let a slow hiss roll off his tongue. Biting his bottom lip slowly, he shook his head. "Not at all, ma, and you already know that shit, so I'm only gon' tell you one last time. Get your little brothers in check, or I'ma have to."

There was a seriousness in Rugga's tone that let me know he really wasn't playing, and shit wasn't a game anymore.

"Alright, babe, I got it. Speaking of, I need to check on Dennis. I've been out here wrecking my brain over Darren and this bullshit he got himself into and how to get back on his good side that I completely forgot about Dennis."

In a hurried rush, I fidgeted out of Rugga's embrace and scurried to the nightstand where my phone sat. After Dennis had his first manic episode last year, I secretly installed cameras in every room in the house. While I knew my actions were an invasion of his privacy, I didn't completely trust Dennis, and most importantly, I was also afraid of what he might do to himself. I hardly checked the secret Ring camera when I was at home because at least I knew he was in the house either playing his game, drinking, or doing some kind of drugs. However, with me away right now, I was feeling a bit uneasy, and I wanted to ensure he was okay.

I pulled up the Ring app on my phone, and several cameras appeared in the interface. I scrolled through most of them, just casually checking on the house. Everything, including the kitchen, looked untouched, which was expected because all Dennis did was order Uber Eats and DoorDash every fucking day. Finally, I clicked on his room camera, and the video enlarged.

Immediately, I saw Dennis lying on the floor face down, appearing unresponsive. His room was a mess. As expected beer bottles, Pringles bottles, and at least twenty Reese's Pieces wrappers covered the floor. I strained my eyes, looking at the video, waiting for him to get up before I panicked.

"Babe, you good?" Rugga's raspy tone startled me.

My heart started pounding as each second progressed, and he hadn't gotten up.

"Come on, Dennis. Come on, baby bro. Get up!" I urged in a panic.

Rugga's shuffling feet sprang up behind me. "Baby, what's up? Talk to me."

I couldn't find the breath, yet somehow, the words still came out. "It's Dennis. I think... I think he's dead."

a change of heart

Charlene

"Boy, don't question me. Did you forget who's the momma here? I don't have to answer to you," I huffed and puffed as I dismissed my son Devin from further prying into my business. He FaceTimed me about ten minutes ago and was already working on my nerves.

"Just because you're grown doesn't mean you can disappear and not come home for weeks," he stressed, stretching his arms and cracking his knuckles while he sat in front of his computer dressed in a three-piece suit. His shirt was buttoned so damn tight around his neck that it looked like he was two seconds away from choking. Instead of correcting him, I just sighed. It didn't matter how much I begged him to loosen up. He was still my goodie-two-shoes of a corporate lawyer son. The only thing he had in common with his father was success, but other than that, he lacked the swag and finesse of my late husband. It used to bother me, but when I thought about how my two baby sons were pretty much thugs, I started to appreciate how green Devin was.

"Listen, hunny. I don't have any small children. I have no kids to cook for or a husband to tend to. I'm outside, ahhkay, baby. Please believe me!" I playfully ranted as I sat on the bed, running my fingers through my head.

The two-week-old style had my hair crunchy and brittle, mirroring the feel of a Brillo pad. I was in need of a fresh wash, set, and curl on my short mane. Today was the perfect day to get my hair done. Darren was downstairs in the lobby's gym preparing for his game next week, and the weather was pretty moderate for me to hit the town.

"You may not have small children, but you're a grandmother."

"Ahht-ahht. What's that supposed to mean?" I objected.

"It means that you should be home with your grandchildren or taking them out, not missing in action for two weeks straight."

"Yous a damn lie if you think I'm finna be in the house with some toddlers. Absolutely not. My days of raising kids are over. It's all about me right about now!"

Devin sighed. "I know, Ma. I'm just messing with you. You're absolutely right. You raised me, Deon, and Devon to the best of your abilities. You deserve to be outside." He chuckled. "But seriously though, ma, how are you doing? More importantly, what are you doing in LA this long?" he pried.

I figured I'd just tell him the truth. "I met someone." Biting my lip, I waited for his criticism.

"Ok... and?"

"I've been spending time with him out here, and he bought me a condo," I confessed.

"WHAT?" Devin gasped. "You've only been there what... two weeks max. Probably only eleven days."

I chuckled. "Hunny, that's all it takes. At least for a pro like me."

"Ahh, sookie sookie now. Ma, you're a mess."

"Ya daddy was tricking too, this soon as well. Don't get it fucked up."

Devin snickered. "Damn, I miss that man." Silence pursued, yet somehow, I still heard the solace in the air between our lines despite us being five hundred miles away from each other.

"Yeah, I miss him too."

Losing Don was an emotional shift for me. Not only did I lose my ex-husband, but my sons also lost their father and their sense of male leadership, stability, and structure. There was nothing I could do to fill that void for my grown sons, who were fathers themselves.

"Anyway, who's the new guy? Clearly, he's got money, and he's not afraid to spend it."

I twisted my lip dramatically and groaned. "I'm not gon' tell you who, but he is someone you know."

"Really?" Devin's brow raised as he leaned closer in the camera, allowing me to get a look up his nostrils.

"Yeah, and that's all I'm going to say."

Buzz. Buzz. Buzz.

The intercom annoyingly rang off, causing me to spring up from the couch. I slipped into my Crocs and motioned toward the intercom.

"Devin, I'll call you back," I stated before abruptly ending the call and stuffing my phone into my pocket.

At the intercom, I tapped the screen, and the Ring camera revealed a distressed-looking Imani. It was clear she was crying from the dried-up tears plastered under her eyes. My disgrace with her instantly left my body, and I buzzed her in. From the way she presented, I was alarmed. As much as I couldn't stand the little bitch, she was Darren's sister, and my care for him extended to her. Ultimately, she was family and had always been. I was the oldest, so I had to be the bigger person.

I trudged toward the front door and opened it. Imani looked even worse in person. Her eyes were pink. You could tell she cried her entire way here. Her lips were dry and cracking, and her body was jittery. We locked eyes, and she rushed into my arms. Loud groans and moans escaped her mouth as she hyperventilated. Breathing heavy, hard, and rapid, she gripped me tightly, forcing me to fully embrace her.

I held her tight as she continued crying. "Imani, what happened?"

As she broke away from me, she rubbed her eyes with the back of her hand, continuing to whimper. "I need to see Darren. Dennis is dead."

"WHAT? MY BROTHER IS GONE?" Darren roared after Imani broke the news to him. His heart was pounding as sweat rolled down his forehead.

"Yes. That's what it looks like. I called the ambulance fifteen minutes ago, and I'm still on hold," she explained, holding up her phone and increasing the volume. Hold music erupted from the speakers and I could see Imani had been on the phone for the last forty-two minutes.

"What? You live in Marietta? How is that possible?" Darren was finally catching his breath.

"I have no fucking idea, but Crissy is on her way to the house now. She might make it before them."

"Okay, so run this shit back to me."

"No, Darren. I'm just going to show you."

Imani pulled up the Ring App on her phone and tapped on a screen. A large figure was laid out on the floor amid countless bottles and other trash.

"He's been laid out like this for nearly an hour," she explained before pulling her phone back, glaring at it, and typing. "Crissy's walking into the house now. Can you FaceTime her from your phone? I don't want to hang up with the ambulance."

I pulled out my phone. "What's her number?"

"404-770-0000."

I keyed it in and hit the FaceTime button. After two rings, a high yellow girl with big curls answered the phone. I quickly passed it to Imani.

"Mani, he won't wake up, but I have a feeling he's not dead." The inflection in her voice was contrived, as if she were trying to suppress the panic.

"Turn your camera around!" Imani insisted.

In an instant, I watched Imani's face go from slack to tense. Her eyes elevated from damp to wet as she hollered out. Darren rushed to her side and grabbed the phone out of her hand.

"Place two fingers near his neck. Do you feel a pulse?"

I neared closer to Darren, resting my hand on his arm as I caught a glimpse of the FaceTime call. Crissy hovered over Dennis' body, and what really was a millisecond felt like an hour. From the heaviness of both Imani and Darren's breathing, I was afraid myself.

"I feel a pulse. A very faint one, but a pulse nonetheless."

Continuing to rub Darren's arm, I nestled my nose onto the back of his neck. He loved when I did that, and I knew it would comfort him.

"The ambulance just pulled up."

Crissy turned the camera around, and bright flashing lights were blaring from the ambulance truck. From a quick glance, I noticed how grand the driveway appeared, with cobblestone surrounding the sides of the pavement and some of the best lawn work I've ever seen.

"Oh, thank God!" Imani declared as she separated from Darren and wiped her eyes.

"Crissy, please make sure they take care of my brother. We'll be in Atlanta in the next five hours," Darren asserted before passing Imani the phone.

My head jerked back as I looked at Darren with a confused gaze.

"Babe, there's was no way that you'll get a flight in the

next hour to make it to Atlanta in the next five hours."

Darren smirked as his eyes traveled up and down my figure. "We ain't flying commercial today, baby. This is my baby brother we are talking about. We don't have time to waste. We're taking the private jet today!"

My mouth dropped open. "Private jet? You have a private jet?" Even Don didn't own a private jet in his prime. In fact, we only rode one once with Floyd Mayweather Sr. and Jr. Don refused to invest in one himself. Flying first class was good enough for him.

'I don't own one, but I use one from time to time, especially when I need to get somewhere fast."

"Well, excuse me, balla shot caller." I kissed my teeth and bit my bottom lip.

Although it wasn't the most appropriate time, all I could think about was taking his long wood into my mouth and allowing him to fuck my face until his cum trickled down my throat. His young ass knew just how to turn me on.

"Mani, get Rugga and Zion and meet me at the Van Nuys Airport in no later than an hour and a half."

WITHIN TWO HOURS, we were boarding the jet from an elegant entranceway, stepping onto a marble floor inlaid with a medallion mosaic surrounded by gold columns. My mouth dropped as we walked through the sliding door into the main lounge, where luxurious cream sofas were lined up, facing inward on all three sides.

Darren firmly grabbed my hand, which jerked me out of la la land. As much as I tried to maintain my composure, I couldn't. Darren just spent two hundred thousand dollars to get us to Atlanta in enough time to ensure his brother was okay. His being a big spender turned me on, but seeing how much he cared for his family allowed me a deeper glimpse into his heart. If I wasn't certain about anything else, I knew I was falling in love with him — for real this time. Honestly, it was hard not to. Money and luxury aside, Darren had the heart of a teddy bear with a sheer innocence that made him irresistible to me.

"Mommy, wow, look!"

Excitement broke out from behind us. I turned around, and Imani, her son, and her man were browsing the dining room located beyond the living space, subtly separated by a divider embedded with a double-face TV.

"I know Ziony! It's beautiful," Imani belted. "Damn, baby bro, you really outdid yourself. Despite the circumstances, this is some fly shit."

Darren chuckled as he motioned toward Imani, leading the way as I clung to his arm.

"C'mon, it's me, baby! Would you expect any less? As soon as I get my offer from the Lakers, I'm buying one of these babies."

"That's big, bro," Rugga said. This was the first time I heard his voice clearly.

I tried my best not to look too hard at him because I knew all I had to do was bat my lashes, and I could have that nigga if I wanted. From my quick observation after seeing him twice, I could tell he was older than Imani, laying down some good dick, and that he had her ass in check. His silent strength was admirable, and if I weren't so wrapped up in Darren, just to spite Imani, I'd take her man, just as she and her momma took mine.

Shit, a few times, I caught Rugga looking at me, but he never stared too long, which I respected. I could tell he was a loyal nigga despite his natural inclination to notice a beautiful woman. His attraction to me was to be expected, but I didn't plan on doing anything about it. Darren had my attention, and besides, I didn't have the urge of vengeance against Imani anymore. She was just a teenager who fell in love with a sexy, powerful man she'd known her entire life. It was sick on Don's behalf, but I could no longer hold it against Imani, especially if I planned on being with her brother for the long haul.

"Yeah, I'm expected to get about three offers. The NBA Draft is in less than two months. All I got to do is hold this press conference, kill this game next week, and finish out the season well," Darren recited, his pitch high and airy.

I could tell that he was excited to brag to Rugga. It was obvious he looked up to him.

"I'm in my last semester and still on track to graduate. Mother's Day can't come sooner," Darren continued. Yet suddenly, his entire energy changed after he mentioned Mother's Day.

"Graduations always land on Mother's Day weekend for some odd reason. Having to walk down the aisle again without Mommy won't be easy. It never gets easy," Darren confessed, filling the jet with his somber sorrow.

brother to brother

Dice

THE ROOM AT WELLSTAR KENNESTONE HOSPITAL was cold and bright as Imani, me, and the doctor stepped inside. Dennis was lightly snoring and had no idea we were there.

"How's he doing?" Imani sniffled.

The doctor, a middle-aged white guy with rounded frames draped around his face, scrunched his lip and sighed. "Mr. Bleeker's doing well considering the lethal combination of OxyContin, Fentanyl, and Molly found in his system. Your brother's lucky to be alive."

Biting my bottom lip, I scurried over to his bedside and watched my brother sleep silently. Dennis looked incredibly different from the last time I saw him. He was heavier, while his face and neck were full of tattoos. I couldn't believe my baby brother had become everything we both vowed never to become. We both vowed that we'd never be like these Atlanta ass niggas who were on lean and taking all kinds of pills. We vowed we would never tattoo our faces, yet I trembled as I looked at him.

While Imani talked to the doctor, I pulled out my phone. I didn't have much time to actually stay here in Georgia. I needed to be back in Los Angeles in two days to prepare for the press conference and my game, which was in five days. I just needed my brother to wake up so I could talk some fucking sense into him. I needed Dennis to get his fucking act together. We're all we have. It was just me, him and Imani. We may have had money, but we didn't have true guidance, and Imani was doing the best she could.

"When do you think he'll wake up, doc?" Imani asked.

I turned around, eyeing the doctor from his Sperry shoes to his jittery hands he fidgeted with. He inhaled and exhaled as his shoulders slumped. Shrugging, he shook his head from side to side. "The paramedics gave him Narcan, and he woke up for a bit yesterday. He didn't talk to me much. He just went back to sleep. I understand Mr. Bleeker has severe bipolar depression. Being that we have been just fueling his body with fluids, we haven't been giving him any of his meds. Just thought you'd like to know."

"Thank you. Well, since he's conscious, can we wake him up?" I asked.

The doctor looked back and forth at Imani and me and shrugged. "I don't see why not."

"Alright then. I'm waking his ass up," I asserted before

jerking Dennis by the arm. "Bro, wake up," I demanded, continuously nudging him.

Dennis stirred a bit before he met me with a bewildered stare.

"Can I get some alone time with my bro?" I stated.

"Of course, of course," the doctor replied before rushing toward the door. "If you need me, let Nurse Reina know."

Within a second, the door swung back several times before fully closing. He was gone, but Imani was still there, now on the opposite side of Dennis' bed.

"Dennis, you had us terrified." Imani's strained face was a pain to see. Veins poked through her temple as her pinched lips were covered in a scowl. Bent over the rail of his bed, she invaded all of his personal space.

"Mani, give me and Dennis some time alone. We need to talk, brother to brother!"

Dennis huffed and puffed as he wiped drool from the side of his mouth but was otherwise silent.

"Look, Darren. He's my brother too, and we need to talk as well, sibling to sibling," she countered.

I rubbed my hands together and stiffened my jaw. Through the splits of my teeth, I replied, "You can talk to Dennis sibling to sibling when we're done talking man to man." My intense gaze rattled Imani as I watched her fidget as she slowly backed away from the bed. Without further qualms, she exited the room.

I didn't give a fuck if Imani was my sister or the fact that she was my elder. I wasn't fighting for my respect. It was understood, and that was all that mattered.

"Bro, what's good with you?" I directed my rage to

Dennis. His fat bubble-lipped, tattooed-faced ass sat slumped like Humpty fucking Dumpty in the bed. At first, I felt sorry for him, but the fact that it repulsed me to even look at him started to infuriate me.

Dennis snorted as he struggled to sit up. "Nigga, don't be questioning me. You ain't my daddy," he sassed before snorting up a ball of mucus. The sound of snot traveling up his windpipes drove me crazy.

"Look nigga, ain't nobody tryna be yo' fucking daddy. I'm just tryna make sure yo' bitch ass don't die out here off all these fucking drugs. You're out here on some loser-type shit. What the fuck, nigga? Then you faking like you got some type of bipolar depression bullshit. You just a weak ass, bitch ass nigga with no discipline or self-pride."

I was tired of his nasty ass attitude.

"Fuck you, nigga. Don't come in here with that bullshit. I ain't ask you to come here no how!" he spat, his voice all nasally and breathy.

"Losing Momma and Daddy ain't been easy on none of us, especially Imani. She also lost the father of her child. She's over here raising a son, running businesses, and taking care of yo' bitch ass, yet you're making it harder on her."

Imani and I may not have been on the best of terms, but the truth was the fucking truth. My and her issues were separate, and we were going to address them soon, but I refused to sit by and let Dennis take advantage of her. Right was right, and this nigga Dennis was dead-ass wrong.

"I don't need shit from you or Imani. I got my own money, thanks to my daddy. If Imani wants me out so bad,

I'll fucking leave! Now get the fuck out!" he yelled as he raised up more in his seat and rattled the bars on his bed.

I chuckled. "Nigga, all that screaming and playing like you crazy ain't scaring me. You need to TIGHTEN the fuck up. You're young, got your whole life ahead of you, yet you're throwing it away with these fucking drugs."

Dennis lowered his eyes, and something took over his face, a ghoulish glow, something I had never seen in him before. White foam crusted around his mouth. "My momma and my daddy ain't here no mo'. If I gotta be on this earth with you, Imani, her bastard child, and her wack-ass boyfriend, I'd rather be dead. NOW GET THE FUCK OUT!" Dennis' roar was so loud that Imani peeked inside, her eyebrow raised as she eyed us both.

"Y'all good in here?"

I nodded my head as I kissed my teeth. "Yeah, I'm good. Talk some sense into your retarded ass brother. He might need them meds after all," I sneered before storming past her and strutting through the swinging door.

I wasted my fucking time coming up here when I could have been at the gym practicing. Dennis' ass was too far gone in the dumps. There was obviously nothing I could do for his ass. My best bet was to focus on me. I had enough shit going on, anyway.

As soon as I stepped out of the hospital, Charlene was waiting inside a drop-top Audi. She looked good in her Fendi shades, driving the car I'd rented for us this weekend. With my mind made up, I jumped into the car and fastened my seat belt.

"How's your brother, hunny?"

Sucking my teeth, I folded my shoulders. "Man, fuck that nigga. He aiight. There's a change of plans. We're flying back to LA tonight. That nigga doesn't need me."

"I'M NOT A MONSTER. I'm not a woman beater. The truth is, I've been suffering with grief. As many of you may know, I lost my mother and my father in the same year. My mother committed suicide, and my father died from MS. That excuses nothing, but I had to come to terms with the fact that I have some repressed sorrow from my parents' death," I announced, clearing my throat and loosening my tie.

I was surrounded by cameras, lights, and a medium-sized audience of about one hundred USC students. Half of them were my basketball team assistants and coaches, and the other half were members of student body organizations. The president of the student council and other organizations, such as sororities and fraternities, sat in the audience, taking notes.

I turned to my far right and spotted Charlene dressed in a flattering skirt suit. It was cream-colored with an accent of blue stripped along the suit's seams. Charlene looked like Olivia Pope, but she really was my first lady. She winked and blew me a kiss, which gave me the confidence to continue.

"Now that I have accepted the fact that grief has impacted my mental health as well as my brother's and other Black men that look like me on this very campus, I am making it my mission to advocate for mental health services for Black men on the campuses of all universities across the nation, especially ivy-league PWIs like USC."

Claps rang throughout the quaint auditorium. A hand raised in the audience, and my publicist, who was sitting beside me, grabbed the mic from the table podium. "Please stand up, state your name, and ask your question."

"Hello, I am Rachel Caswell, the President of USC's Kappa Alpha Theta chapter. How exactly do you plan to advocate for mental health services for Black men?"

I picked back up my mic and smiled before speaking. This was an exercise my publicist made me practice over and over to ensure I was ready for this conference over the last week. She instructed me to always smile before I spoke because it painted me as warm and allowed my nerves to rest.

"I'm glad you asked Rachel because I am very excited about the partnership I have with Black Men Cry, the nation's leading mental health organization providing affordable mental health services for Black men."

"That sounds great and all, but mental health affects everyone. Not just men, and certainly not just Black men. Second, with a Black population of less than 6% at USC and an even smaller population of Black males, how at all does this partnership or push for mental health services for Black men benefit USC? Can you please make it make sense for me?" she asked in a snickering tone which irritated the shit out of me.

As I watched her obnoxious mouth move, I recognized where I remembered her from. Rachel was a pass-around slut, that fucked the entire basketball team. She was the bitch that got gang-banged for fun. Her father was on the board of Google and Salesforce, so she came from money, Silicon Valley money. She wasn't just a whore. She was a trick, too, and she hated the fact that I never fucked her or even let her hoe ass suck my dick. The bitch offered me ten thousand dollars to suck my dick, and I still turned her down, and she hated me for it.

Unlike my boy Ace who let her pay him to fuck her, I didn't need the money. And besides, I never trusted those white sluts. They were the type to call rape if you didn't obey them. Keeping my distance from her was the best thing I could have done. No one could ever place us together. I didn't even go to parties she or her crew were at. Those snow bunnies were scandalous as fuck, and because they came from powerful families, anyone would believe them, especially over my Black ass.

I took a deep breath, although I was lost for words. My publicist, Susan, noticed and stepped in. Grabbing the additional mic from the table, she stood up from her seat.

"With Darren being the face of Black Men Cry, by association, USC is supporting an important cause that will only put USC in a caring light relating to mental health. Either way, it's a win-win and costs the university nothing," Susan expressed through a sincere smile.

"Yeah, it sounds like a win-win for you and your client but not for USC or the student body. It just sounds like a great cover-up to hide the perpetual abuse against Black women," Rachel countered.

No the fuck she didn't just use the violence against

Black women as her ploy. I was livid and just hoping it wasn't etched across my face. As I looked into the audience and found the few Black female faces, I settled in on the president of Delta Sigma Theta, the most prominent Black sorority on USC's campus. She looked appalled and turned her head to face Rachel. With her arms folded, I knew she was on my side. Before I could respond, she raised her hand and stood up quickly. Rocking long silky tresses that touched her waist and wispy bangs that she swept out of her face, she rolled her eyes as she walked over to Rachel. Snatching the microphone from her hand, she sighed.

"Rachel, in the most respectful and humble way possible, neither myself nor other Black women need you to speak for us. In fact, I'd love to hear more about the partnership with Black Men Cry. Darren, can you tell us more? What services does Black Men Cry offer, and how will you participate?" the Delta asked, with the brightest smile I had ever seen and heard through someone's teeth.

lost ones

Imani

"THERE'S NO WAY YOU ARE REALLY CONTEMPLATING on having Dennis stay here, especially after his ass overdosed," Rugga argued. "He needs to be in rehab!"

Rugga was stating the obvious, but I had already had the talk with Dennis about rehab, and he cursed me the fuck out. He said he wasn't going to no fucking rehab, and there was nothing I could do to make him. He also told me that if I wanted him out, all I had to do was say the word, and he'd be gone.

We were back in our Marietta home, arguing once again. This time, I was stuck between a rock and a hard place because months ago, all I wanted was for Dennis to leave, but now, more than ever, I wanted him to stay. I needed him to stay under my care. I couldn't leave him to feign for himself because if anything happened to my baby brother, I'd never forgive myself.

"I already told you. Dennis is not going to rehab, and I can't make him."

Rugga was shirtless, his washboard abs tighter than ever as he rubbed his hands together. "You can't make his punk ass do shit, and it's really starting to annoy the fuck out of me. You're letting this little nigga run our house, and I'm sick of it! I'm the only man of this house!"

I cut my eyes at Rugga, my sharp gaze piercing through his chest. I stood up from the bed and placed my hands on my hips.

"I'm not arguing with you tonight about this shit. Let's not forget that this is my house! You may pay property taxes and see that shit gets taken care of around here, but the only person's name on this deed is Imani Bleeker. Not to mention, my last name is Bleeker, and yours is Stapleton. Until my last name changes to yours, you will never have the last word in here, especially as it relates to my family." I was breathing hard, and my chest was heaving. "And if you don't like it, you can leave."

As soon as the words left my mouth, I instantly regretted them. Rugga's eyes widened as his shoulders drooped. His neck was bent, and his upper lip was snarled.

"Say less. I'ma make you stand on that shit, too."

Without saying another word to me, he stormed to the closet and pulled out a large Nike duffle bag. He began ripping items off the hangers and folding them before dumping them into the bag.

I rushed behind him, resting my hand on his arm. He

yanked away quickly without even looking at me. His rejection jarred me to a place I hadn't visited in a long time — abandoned, desolate, left to the waste side just as Don's death positioned me. Without love, without my companion, and without my friend.

Holding back tears, I bit down hard on my lips. "Rugga." I mustered.

He remained silent. Just the thrusting and tussling of fabric meshing against cloth permeated our silence.

"RUGGA!" I yelled.

Nothing.

I tugged on his arm, and that's where I jerked a reaction.

"WHAT, IMANI? WHAT!"

Squeezing my chest together as I twiddled my thumbs, I raised my head despite the hurt I felt. I had to face him.

"Where are you going?"

He turned to me abruptly, the duffle bag in one hand and a shirt in another. "Look, we need some space. You got a lot going on with your brothers, and I think it would be best if you handle that shit solo. Forreal, ma." Rugga's cold eyes stared a black hole into my chest. It was as if he was seeing right through me.

I felt like my oxygen was being cut off. I couldn't lose Rugga, too, not at this vulnerable time when I needed him the most.

"But you can't go. I need you," I pleaded.

Rugga chuckled as he sucked his teeth. "No, you don't. You made that clear. Now I'm gon' leave you to handle ya business. I'll be at my condo in Buckhead. I'll check on you in a few days," he stated before kissing my forehead. He vanished in a quickness, but his scent stayed with me.

I found the nearest wall, slid down, crunched into a ball, and cried my eyes out.

I was all alone on this planet with a world of problems and no one to help. No parents, the matriarch of a family, responsible for three humans, not including myself. I was losing my brothers, one to disease and addiction and the other to a conniving, gold-digging bitch, and now I lost my man.

I wiped my face, stumbled to the nightstand, and grabbed my phone. I had to try with Darren. I couldn't lose him to Charlene. He was my favorite, and I needed his help with Dennis. I dialed him up, and he answered on the fourth ring before the voicemail.

"What's up, Imani?" he spoke coldly into the phone.

I swallowed my pride, and I exhaled. "I need your help with Dennis and your commitment to bettering our relationship. We're all we got. We have to stay tight regardless of who we are dating."

There wasn't complete silence on the other end of the line. I heard his breathing clearly.

It was bright outside as the sun dawned on my room, but still inside, I felt dreary.

"Aiight, sis. I got you. I'ma see when I can shoot out to Atlanta. And you're right. We're siblings. These bitches and niggas come and go. We're locked in for life."

My heart skipped a beat as his compliance restored my hope. I needed that.

"That's fucking right. For life, baby. What did Momma always say?"

"BLEEKER FOUND, BLEEKER BOUND!" we both yelled in unison.

"Damn, I miss that ole crazy lady." Darren sighed.

"I miss her too."

I was now sitting up in my bed Indian style, my chest erect, feeling a tad bit confident. It's amazing what love could do to you in an instant. Real, pure, genuine love is electrifying.

"Remember when she left us at the rest stop in California?"

"How could I ever forget it? She was so mad at us that she left our asses and only took Dennis," Darren reminisced.

I sat back, thinking of that day. Daddy was out of the country and couldn't come on our planned vacation. Momma, being her defiant self, decided to still take us to Universal Studios in Florida. Darren and I wandered off for hours somewhere in the park. When Momma finally found us, she was so upset that she refused to travel with us. She gave us each one hundred dollars, two bus tickets, and our bookbags with clothes in them and told us since we wanted to be grown to take the bus from California to Atlanta. She said not to call her, and she'd be there to pick us up. Meanwhile, she and Dennis, who was no more than four or five years old at the time, flew back home.

"Those were the scariest two days of my life," I confessed.

"Mine too, but we had each other and made it through

together, just like we will now. You know, Momma taught us some valuable lessons and prepared us for some real-life shit. It's as if she knew she was gonna go, and she needed us to experience that." Darren was onto something.

I relaxed into the bed, pulling my fleece blanket over me and wiggling my toes as I listened to my baby brother speak so poetically and profoundly. It was refreshing because he was right.

"Yeah, one of those lessons was to never fall asleep on the bus because, baby, those people on that bus were unpredictable. In the name of Jamie Foxx, bro," I joked.

"No bullshit, sis," Darren agreed.

"It was nice talking to you, bro. You don't know how much I needed this," I admitted.

"You don't know how much I needed this too, sis. Don't worry, we locked in. I'll hit you no later than tomorrow about my flight schedule."

A giddy feeling rolled from my belly to behind my ears. "I love you, bro."

"I love you too, sis."

I hung up the phone, feeling accomplished. It felt good to settle that shit with Darren earlier than later. We had enough on our plate with Dennis anyway, and I knew I couldn't handle his ass by myself. Darren was the perfect person to get his brother in shape. I looked at the time and noticed it was close to two p.m. I hopped up and started to get ready. Zion was getting out of school soon, and since I hadn't gone to the boutique since I'd been back from LA these last few days, the least I could do was be on time to pick him up.

BY THE TIME I was dressed and downstairs, I was met by Dennis with his shirt off and, a blunt in his mouth and one behind his ear.

"Didn't I tell your ass no smoking in my house? In your room only!" I barked.

My skin was hot, so I knew my blood was boiling. Just the sight of Dennis infuriated me. Part of me was heartbroken, disappointed, and saddened for my parents. Darren and I had our demons, but Dennis' were eating him alive. Everything went downhill as soon as Mommy died. Looking at Dennis reminded me of our trauma, of the generational curses we inherited.

Dennis looked at me, not saying a word. He inhaled a long pull of his weed and blew it out before chuckling.

I sped up, storming toward him. "You think this shit is funny, huh?" I roared, hitting him repeatedly in the back with my fists.

In a quickness, my head jerked in the opposite direction, and before I knew it, Dennis was wailing on top of me, hitting me in the face viciously, again and again. I struggled to block his blows. His fist crushed my eye continuously. I cried out until I couldn't feel the nerves in my eye anymore. For what felt like an eternity finally stopped as Dennis got off me.

"Learn to keep your hands to your fucking self!" he spat before turning around and walking off.

CHAPTER FOURTEEN

announcement

Charlene

"WE'RE PLAYING BASKETBALL. WE LIKE THAT basketball."

The timeless tune rang throughout the gymnasium, startling me at first. Crowds of girls were dancing and shaking away as the cheerleaders welcomed the Trojans onto the floor. These kids were twenty-five and younger. They didn't know shit about Kurtis Blow, but as soon as the beat dropped, another rapper, most likely someone from their age group, blared through the speakers and they sang along word for word.

I stood near the coach's den in my Prada heeled sandals, skinny jeans draping my thighs, a crop leather jacket on my arms, and some Aviator sunglasses sitting on the tip of my nose. Classic chic at its finest. Sassy, sexy, and mature yet youthful and full of life. Darren was huddled up with his team, stealing a look at me every second he could. Catching my gaze, he licked his lips and blinked seductively. I could feel his tension even with him being at least thirty feet away from me.

His seductive stare intensified the heat in the gymnasium. We were looking at each other so intently that neither of us noticed when the game started until the players were sprinting back and forth across the court. Darren nearly trampled over his own foot but quickly regained his footing.

I sat down in my floor seat and crossed my legs. Instead of watching the game, I glanced around the gym, looking for agents and scouts we needed to know. One quick whiff to the right revealed Boshini Tyler, the leading scout for The Golden Nuggets. A few rows below him to the far left was Nav Locil, the head scout for the Miami Heat.

Darren was right. All the heavy hitters were here tonight, and his future rode on this very game. Lost in my thoughts, I didn't fully hear the excitement of the gym. I quickly raised my head, and there was a short, obese, brown-skinned girl staring at me. With hands on her hips, dressed in a tight spandex two-piece set and some slides, her wig was lifting, and I could tell she hadn't had a pedicure in months.

Damn. These young bitches look bad and got the nerve to be staring at someone.

I turned my face to the left, and her eyes followed me. She scooted her body over, so there was no way I could avoid looking at her. I pulled out a stick of gum and chewed a few times until I blew out a bubble. I could feel her eyes burning a hole in me. That's when I knew it had to be none other than Tati, Darren's ex-girlfriend. The same bitch that got him in this bullshit with USC. *Why the fuck was she here at his game?*

Twiddling my thumbs, I turned my face from her, directing my gaze to the center of the floor. The intensity ran from the player's face down their shoulders to their hands, calves, and feet. They were bolting with lightning, ready to expel the thunder on each other. Darren had the ball, guarding it with his life as he stumbled down the court, bouncing the Spalding every other second, swishing it from his right to his left hand, under his legs, and around his torso. He made it down the court with some struggle but leaped into a slam dunk.

The gym went crazy. Hoots, hollers, claps, and stomps bounced from wall to wall as young girls were twerking back and forth. The MC dropped a snippet of Sexyy Red's latest smash, and everyone yelled out "Ske Yee!" at the top of their lungs. The energy was electrifying even after the music was cut.

I inched up into my seat, watching the game eagerly and proudly clapping whenever Darren scored until the very last seconds of the game. It seemed like Darren owned the ball, and again, he had it. The Trojans were up by one point, and only twelve seconds were left in the game. I don't know how he managed to catch a three-pointer mid-court, but he did, and the game ended with the Trojans as the victor. "Ske Yee" by Sexyy Red came on again, and this time, everyone, including me, rose from their seats and began cheering.

Gathering my bag, I shuffled toward the team and met eyes with Darren right away. With a towelette in my hand, I rushed in his direction. Before I could pass him the towel, he grabbed me into his arms and kissed me deeply. Sweat fell from his forehead as he firmly gripped my ass. Nibbling on my lip a little longer than usual, I could taste the sweat from his mouth, and instantly my pussy lips slid against each other. He finally let me go, and I wiped his face with the towel.

"Good game, baby! Congrats on another win!"

He smirked. "Thank you, baby!"

Grabbing my hand into his, Darren motioned me through the crowd of attendees. Never bothering to join his team, he strutted out with me as the game watchers chanted his name continuously. "Dice! Dice! Dice!"

Tucking me under his arm, I got a whiff of his earthly musk, and the hairs on my neck rose. Flashing lights from the cameras of school photographers and paparazzi brightened my face. Thank God for my shades.

Out of nowhere, a young Black girl, no older than thirty-five years old, dressed in a suit, approached us with a cameraman and a mic.

"Tanasia Thompson with MSNBC covering all NCAA news and events. Just a few words, Dice. Please?" she begged.

"Sure," he agreed, still catching his breath.

I tried to pull away to give him his space to interview, but he grabbed me closer to him, sharing the camera with me. I smiled lightly, thankful that my shades were concealing my eyes. Shocked, I pursed my lips to hide my nervousness.

"You did great out there, carrying the team with 72 points. How does it feel to come back from such an unfortunate viral incident to such a big win like tonight's?"

Darren tilted his head to the side and scratched his chin before exhaling. Grabbing the mic into his hand, he responded, "It truly feels like a blessing to come back strong as I did. I'm blessed." He kept it short and sweet.

"Thank you so much, Dice. Last question. What got you here? What got you through that difficult time to scoring 72 points on your first game back?"

Darren smiled and squeezed me tighter. "It's really who got me through that difficult time. This woman you see right here is responsible for motivating me, understanding me, and looking out for my best interest."

The reporter's face beamed with light. "And does this woman have a name, Dice?" she asked, looking back and forth at us.

"Yeah, her name is mine. Now, thank you for your time," Darren stated before tugging me away from the reporter.

Darren gripped my hand tighter as we navigated through the crowd, bogarting the exit and ensuring the coast was clear before pushing open the gym's side doors. As we reached the end of the building, a few feet away from the cars, Tati reappeared. This time, she wore sweats and sneakers, and her terrible wig was wrapped in a ponytail.

"So, you sporting this old bitch around campus now?" Tati barked.

Darren pulled me back by the arm and stepped in front of me. "Don't embarrass yourself out here, girl. You and I are done! Stop fucking stalking me!" he spat, now pulling me by the arm, yanking me toward the parking lot.

Tati followed up behind us, and I could also hear the commotion from the crowd following as well.

"Look, little girl. I'm gon' tell you this once and once only. Don't you bring ya big ass up on me because I won't hesitate to knock you the fuck out," I threatened, my hands on my hips, standing side by side with Darren.

"Chill, baby, chill," Darren urged. "I got this."

"Tati, hear me clearly. You and I are over. Nothing you say or do can change that. Have some fucking shame and do your fucking hair. Don't let yourself go and try to blame me for it."

Tati was mute, with pain etched across her face. "So that's how you gon' do me, Dice? Just turn your back on me cold for some older bitch you just met? What about us and everything we've been through? Everything we built?"

Truly, it hurt to see this young girl crying, begging, and pleading for a man to be with her who clearly wasn't interested.

"Tati, what we had is over, and what we built can be built with others. God bless you." Those were the last words Darren spoke before we both jolted across the parking lot and jumped into his Audi. Within minutes, we had forgotten all about the fiasco and were grooving to some early 2000s R&B vibing exactly how we should be.

standing on business

Dice

IT WAS THE FIRST DAY OF APRIL. APRIL FOOLS' DAY, and I just touched down at Hartsfield-Jackson International Airport in the heart of my city, Atlanta, Georgia. Well, really, College Park because if you're from the A, you know the airport is out south, not too far from Old National Highway.

The sun was shining, and a pleasant stench of mischief was in the air that always welcomed the start of Atlanta's summer, which kicked off the first week of April and ended on Halloween, sometimes even Thanksgiving. It just depended on what was really in the air. I had one small suitcase because I hadn't planned on staying longer than two weeks. Luckily, I could complete my homework online, and finals weren't until the end of the month.

Things had finally started to calm down at USC.

Attention was no longer on the viral incident. The entire campus was consumed with preparing for finals, graduation and its accompanying activities. Practice was going well, and I had personally met with three scouts who pitched their offers to me — lots of endorsement promises, team-specific perks, and Hollywood associations. Miami Heat, Golden State, and the Houston Rockets approached me. The Lakers still hadn't, and neither did the Celtics, so I couldn't give in yet. We still had two months until the draft, so I had to wait it out. Damn, I wish Momma were here. She would have told me what to do.

Nonetheless, Charlene's been holding me down. In fact, she was the one who told me to hold out until I got five offers before even thinking of who to commit to. As I stepped out of the airport, my cell phone rang.

"What's up, baby? I'm here near S4."

"I see you, baby. Stay right there. I'm pulling up."

In less than a minute, Charlene had pulled up in a clean, olive-colored Cherokee Grand Sport. It was the perfect day for this car. Charlene told me her car collection was sick, but I didn't believe her. It had been a week since I last saw her, the only time we've spent apart in the last three months. I asked Charlene to go back to Atlanta while I closed out some things. I made sure Tati was out of the first condo, and I got it in shape for the property manager to take over for Airbnb hostings. I needed to handle that alone. It was my true closure to everything with Tati.

I hopped into the car, and Charla's sweet perfume hit me. We exchanged a warm kiss as I gripped her inner thigh. She bit on my bottom lip, and my wood bulged.

"I missed you, baby," she cooed as she wiped the love drool off the side of her mouth.

"I missed you too. You just don't know how much, but I promise before the night ends, I'ma show ya ass," I flirted.

Charla chuckled. "So, babe, where's your first stop? Imani's? Food? You hungry?"

"Yeah, I'm hungry for some of you. Take me home, baby. We'll order in."

Charla's giddy laugh invaded the car, and she pressed hard on the gas, and we sped off down I-285. The wind slapped my face and shoulders, and I can't lie. It felt hella good to be back home, even if only for a little while. From the way Charla was rubbing my balls, I knew she was ready for me to empty the clip.

WE STUMBLED into the house almost two hours later after two frozen patron margaritas each. We'd stopped at the Mexican spot in the gas station and picked up some food instead. The drinks got to us, and by the time we entered her house, we were jumping out of our clothes. Charlene's home was modernly lavish, and you could tell she took pride in her linen, furniture, and scents.

After she kicked off her heeled sandals, I picked her up in my arms.

She giggled as I tickled her on her belly. As I walked about the house, remembering it briefly from the last time I was here, I wound up in the living room.

"Ma, what the fuck?" A mid-height loser type nigga who looked like Trippie Redd asked with bewildered dark eyes.

"Babe, hold on. Let me down," Charlene directed me. As she fidgeted out of my arms, she landed feet first on the floor. Without her heeled sandals, she was much shorter than me.

"Devon, what the hell are you doing here?"

"Uhh, the question is, who the hell is this nigga? He looks younger than me when I was twenty-five."

I made the decision to let his comment slide as I raised my head to face him fully. The more and more I looked at him, the more and more I saw Dennis in him. I squinted my eyes a bit and cleared my vision to make sure that I wasn't just getting lost in the face tattoos.

"Devon, don't worry about who I'm with. I said you could stay here for a few days. Your ass was supposed to be gone by noon to avoid all this shit. It's almost six o'clock, so I'm going to ask you again: WHAT ARE YOU DOING HERE?"

He violently flinched and scrunched his nose. "Don't be yelling at me in front of this nigga! You done lost yo' rabbit ass mind!"

My wrists were shaking as I balled up my fists. After rocking back and forth twice, I made the decision, and before I knew it, Charla's son was knocked out cold on the floor. I stared down at him, studying all the features of his face. He really did look like Dennis, and I even saw a bit of myself in him. It was weird.

"BABE, why the fuck would you do that?" Charlene screamed, directing her fury at me.

"If I talked to my mother that way, she would have pulled a knife out of me. No bullshit. I'm not finna sit up here and tolerate this nigga disrespecting my lady. I don't give a fuck that he's your son. Respect my woman in my presence or pay the consequences. It's that simple," I asserted as I cracked my knuckles.

Charla looked at me, puzzled. I could see the hesitation buried in her brows before she completely softened her face.

"Next time, can I get a warning, babe? Like before you knock out one of my sons, can there be an argument first, so I know wassup?" she lightheartedly joked.

"Alright, you got it," I said as I grabbed her by the hand, and we shimmied out of the living room. Before exiting, I turned around and saw her son still lying on the floor. "He'll be just fine in about an hour or two. Don't worry."

In a matter of five minutes, I got Charlene up the stairs, where the fire returned. Passion was riddled all over Charla's face as she rode me wildly, massaging all the corners of her walls on my shaft. Just a few weeks ago, we took off the condom and haven't looked back since. Since Charla had full-on menopause, we didn't have to worry about her getting pregnant. On top of that, we both got tested two weeks ago and were both in the clear for any STDs or STIs. Leaving Tati's nagging ass, who stayed with a case of BV or a yeast infection, for a fine ass, always horny, always sucking, fucking, and cooking cougar was the best thing I ever did.

I was becoming a man, and only a sophisticated woman with Charla's grace and experience could come with. No if ands, or buts. Now, that's what you call standing on business.

I WOKE up refreshed and to the smell of some ole country cooking. Squinting my eyes and stretching my arms, I restored myself before heading to the bathroom. Visions of Charla's face as she bounced on my dick with a rhythm and smoothness flashed through my mind. I hurried up and showered, dressed, and headed downstairs straight for the kitchen. Passing the living room, I saw it was spic and span, and no sign of the scuffle between me and Charla's son was present.

I turned into the kitchen, and Charlene was wearing a black negligee with a heart cut out and a bow sitting at the crack of her ass. Her legs were oiled and shiny, and her pedicured feet sat inside some tall, heeled sandals. She stood over the stove with a spatula in her hand, and my dick stiffened as I motioned her way. She turned to me, and the brightest set of teeth shined. She had the most beautiful smile I'd ever seen, and the dents in her dimples reflected a bright glow that made her simply irresistible.

"Breakfast is ready. This is my last pancake, babe," Charlene informed me before I grabbed her lips into mine and smacked her ass. She nearly stumbled, but I caught her quickly, gripping her into a protective embrace and nibbling on her ear.

"It smells good in here, baby," I complimented as I

watched her place the last pancake onto the stack on the plate and cut the stove off.

"Thanks, baby. What are you getting into today?"

As I held her by the waist, rocking steadily, my chin resting on her shoulder, I said, "After I eat, I'm headed over to Imani's. I got to see what's good with this nigga, Dennis."

"Right, right, okay. Sounds good. I'm going to do a little shopping and pampering today. I'm gonna hit the spa and shop for myself and the house. I also have a meeting with my business manager. She has an opportunity for me that could be very lucrative."

Just the way she talked got a rise out of me. She was sure of herself, ambitious, and still feminine. That shit turned me on so much that I bent her over and dropped my pants to my ankles. Viciously, I ripped off a piece of the negligee as I slid deep inside of her. My long, thick cock invaded her heavenly walls, parting between her honey. Intoxicating moans escaped her mouth as I held her by the back of her waist and pounded into her peach.

"Mhmm, mhmm. Yes, daddy!" she purred.

The inside of her pussy fit around my dick like a glove. She pulled her left ass cheek back, holding it with her hand while I got inside her real good. As open as she was, I now felt all of her. Vibrating my tool around every crevice of her walls, I grunted, surprised at how quickly I was on the verge of busting.

Charlene tightened her walls and jerked back, speeding up her tempo as she threw that fat ass onto me.

"ARRGH!" I shouted as I went into power drive on her pussy.

Beating up her cheeks quickly at a consistent rhythm, touching the back of her insides, and rearranging her guts, I finally slowed up. As I withdrew my dick, it was dripping with cum that was floating somewhere in Charla's stomach.

AFTER EATING and cleaning myself up, I hopped into Charlene's 2008 Lexus and made my way to Imani's. Although I had more than enough money to rent a car, it was a nice gesture for Charla to offer one of her cars. It showed me she really fucked with me and was willing to share with me as well. After hearing Imani call her a gold digger, it'd always been in the back of my mind haunting me. I occasionally wondered if Charlene was a gold digger. The only conclusion I came to was if this was how a gold digger treated you, I was all in.

In less than an hour, I pulled up to the house and rang the bell. A distressed and tired Imani came to the door wearing sweats and a bonnet. I checked my Apple watch for the time. It was after ten o'clock in the morning.

"Wake the fuck up, sis! Ain't you supposed to be getting ready for work?" I greeted her with open arms. "Why the fuck do you got shades on in the house?" I questioned.

She shrugged and didn't say a word. Refusing to give into her wallows or even press her about wearing shades early in the morning, I grabbed her into a tight, playful embrace and pressed my knuckles into her back. She cracked a hesitant smile and squirmed in my arms.

"Stop, Darren," she argued.

"Nah, you stop. Your favorite brother is here to save the day. Put a smile on your face. Tighten the fuck up," I asserted as I walked into the house, pulling her along with me.

Imani's house was a complete one-eighty from Charlene's. They had completely different tastes. Imani's style was lavish, modern, and over the top. Charlene's was more subtle, classic nevertheless still expensive.

We passed by the elaborate fish tank that I've always been mesmerized with, and Imani fidgeted out of my embrace.

"FYI, I'm not going to work today."

I looked at her and scoffed. It seemed like every time I spoke to her, she wasn't at work.

"I'm the boss, remember? I don't have to be there every day," she defended my silent thoughts, standing with her arms on her invisible hips that were buried in oversized gray sweats.

"Yeah, yeah. Follow me," I asserted as I walked through the house toward Dennis' room. Without quarreling, Imani followed.

I took a deep breath as I neared his door. Knocking twice, without waiting, I barged in. As expected, Dennis was asleep, sprawled out, face down on the bed. His obnoxious snore was hard to ignore, so we knew the nigga wasn't dead. At least ten bottles were thrown about the floor, accompanied by a stench of booze and greasy food.

I looked back at Imani, and her pursed, duck lips and folded arms told me all I needed to know. Several lava lights were spread out across the room, along with black curtains along the wall, preventing any lick of sunlight. I eyed the wall outlets and saw that colored lightbulbs were in two of them. I fumed, with nostrils flaring, rubbing my hands together before finding the light switch on the wall.

I flicked on the light, and the room illuminated brightly. Rushing to his side of the bed, I pulled out my phone, found the Clock app, and clicked on the Alarm sound. I placed the phone directly near his ear and let it sound off as I jerked him viciously out of his sleep.

"WAKE UP, NIGGA! WAKE THE FUCK UP!"

A groggy Dennis perked up, wiping drool from the side of his mouth and crust from around his eyes.

"What the fuck, bro?" Dennis roared as he jumped up, revealing a bare chest and saggy man tits.

"That's right, nigga. Get the fuck up, and let's hit the fucking gym. You're not 'bout to kill yourself on my fucking watch. Hustle nigga, let's go!" I ordered.

Dennis looked back and forth at Imani and me and sighed.

"Bro, it's not an option. Your fat ass is working out. Either the easy way, or you gon' have to fight me, nigga. You know you can't beat me, so what's it gon" be?" Now I was up on him, my breath on his face, and I meant every fucking word I said. And if he tests me, I won't hesitate to make him a believer.

my man, my man, my man

Imani

"Y'ALL HAVE NO IDEA HOW BIG OF A HELP DARREN has been with Dennis in just a few short days," I sighed before taking a bite out of the best lemon pepper wings in Atlanta.

The entire gang was together today, and we were having lunch at Suite Lounge. Secluded in a circular velvet booth, we had just enough privacy to do some heavy catching up. To the left of me was my best friend, Crissy. To the left of Crissy was TT, my business partner bestie, and his twin sister Shima. It'd been months since we were last all together, and it was exactly what I needed. A night out with the girls.

"That's really good to hear, girl, especially since that means Dennis is doing better," Crissy responded.

"Yeah, better than I've seen him in years. I wish Darren

could stay. He has such a great influence on Dennis."

TT, dressed in a black sheer top with flair wrists, picked up his cocktail and took a quick sip. "I'm glad the boys aren't fighting anymore, and you can get some peace in your house. What's up with Rugga? When is he coming back home, and when is your ass coming back to work?" TT sassed.

"That's right, brother, business first. Get in that ass." Shima, who was wearing a two-piece short set, butted in.

"Nobody asked for your two cents," I playfully snarled at Shima, yet still rolled my eyes.

It was no secret. She was my least favorite of the bunch. In fact, Shima was the only one that I didn't talk to outside of the group. We rarely communicated separately unless it was to surprise TT for his birthday or if we were all together and TT's phone was dead, or he was out of reach. The truth is, we outgrew each other long ago, and she was just around due to association. I wish I could say decoration, but she didn't exactly look like much.

"Anyway, TT." I sighed dramatically. "Rugga ain't answering my calls. He's texting me, though. Short shit like 'you good?' 'everything alright?', but he's purposely ignoring my calls."

"You think, bitch? That man is tired of you and your brother's shit. He doesn't mind being a step daddy to Zion, but taking on Dennis is a lot," TT objected. "And on top of that, you ain't been listening to your man. At this point, it's really him or Dennis, and you're choosing your brother."

TT's words hit a sore spot. It was true. In all actuality, I was choosing Dennis simply because he's my brother, one of the two only family members I had, which shouldn't even need to be explained to my best friend.

"Well, Rugga's gon' have to get over it. My brothers are all I have, end of the story. However, I am willing to let go in some areas. The truth is, I'm tired of dealing with Dennis. Just because he's doing good now doesn't mean I forgot about him attacking me."

"Girl, what? He attacked you?" Crissy protested.

TT and Shima were both sitting on the edge of their seats. Shima was biting her nails, and TT's eyes were bulging and wide.

"I pushed that shit so far in the back of my mind that I hadn't told a soul. Not even Darren knows. I'm sure if he did, he would fuck Dennis up. I just don't want the drama now or to disrupt the peace."

"So you're here dumping it all on us instead of Darren, who could actually do something about it? Who do we thank for the pleasure?" TT joked. "No, but seriously girl, Dennis' ass has got to go. Not only is he fucking up your relationship, but he's also fucking up your face, sweety." TT giggled as he pinched my cheek several times. "I see those bruises underneath that blush, sweety."

That's when I lost it. Usually, I would be down for TT's dark humor and sarcastic banter, but he had gone too far.

"IT'S NOT FUCKING FUNNY!" I screamed before tearing off my sunglasses, revealing an eyepatch that covered my left eye.

Shima plopped back into the velvet booth and covered her mouth. "Oh my god, girl. I am so sorry."

"Mani, your eye! That's it. You need to press charges,"

Crissy insisted.

I picked up my empty glass of water, slurped the ice into my mouth, and chewed on it. I kept bags of ice in my house simply to chew whenever I felt anxious or nervous.

"No, I'm not pressing charges. My eye will be just fine. It just needs a few weeks to heal. I clean it twice a day. It's just swollen and healing. I'll be just fine."

TT reached over Crissy and grabbed my wrist. "Girl, you are out of your fucking mind. You're wearing a fucking eyepatch. You need to tell Rugga. Let your man step to Dennis' low-life ass. See if he'll beat on him how he beat on you," TT fumed.

"As harsh as it sounds, I'm with TT on this one. Something has to give. Dennis has to pay for putting his hands on you. I'll never understand, after all you do for him, how he has the audacity to raise a finger at you."

I rolled my eyes and folded my arms. "Dennis is not in his right mind and hasn't been since my parents passed. Between that, his bipolar depression, and all those drugs he's been taking instead of his meds, Dennis ain't right, y'all. He refuses to go to rehab, and I'm tired of fighting with him," I confessed nothing more than the truth. "Fighting with him is tiring. I just want peace in my life, and since Darren's been around, I've seen dramatic changes in Dennis."

Silence pursued after I poured my heart out until the grinding of TT's teeth filled the circle.

"And what happens when Darren goes back to LA? What then? Will you still tolerate Dennis beating your ass? Come on, girl. Be real with yourself," TT ranted.

I turned my head, facing Crissy, whose lips were pursed, accompanied by her elbow on the table and a snarl on her face. She rolled her neck and nodded without saying a word. I knew Crissy was fed up. Being my most level-headed friend of the bunch, not much ticked Crissy off. She was a true ride-or-die, hence why she was married, and I wasn't. She had a coolness about her that allowed her to dominate her emotions and stay leveled. When Crissy meant business, she was quiet, so I knew she was completely in agreement with TT. With TT, he just always said the things you needed to hear in the most direct and, might I add, crude way.

"Look, I can't speak to the future, but what I know NOW is that we, my family and me, are working through it, so I don't need no judgment, no badgering or any of that bullshit from you three. You're my safe haven. I need support and understanding from you."

Shima's face was flushed with shock. Crissy's mouth was soft, but TT had his duck lips poked out and his extra side eye on lean, looking at me with a hint of annoyance.

"Well, I'll definitely support ya, girl, but I don't think I can understand all that baby. What I will say is you need to go get your man. Trust me, he'll understand!" TT clicked his tongue, picked up his half-empty cocktail, and threw it back. "Woo baby, after all that, I needed something with a kick. You sho' is a mess, girl."

Mouth half open, I looked at him with a strained eye and sucked my teeth. "Fuck you."

"Ouu hunny, you know I don't swing that way, but nice

try." TT snickered as he rolled his eyes at me and jerked his neck.

Girls' night wasn't going as smoothly as I was hoping. Still, what did I expect after revealing that Dennis beat me so badly that I was wearing an eyepatch? The doctors told me I was lucky I didn't lose my eye and that it would take a few weeks for it to fully heal. Once healed, the doctors also told me my eye may be sensitive to light, which could lead to headaches and further complications. I didn't share all that with my friends because they would have panicked more than expected, and they truly had my best interest at heart. They just all showed it in different ways.

As much as I couldn't stand Shima, she was actually the most compassionate and the least judgmental. She allowed me to vent without forcing her opinions on me or telling me what to do. That was the exact kind of support I needed from a friend while I was going through all this shit. I just needed someone to listen because I knew, in the grand scheme of things, that there would come a point where I would have to separate from Dennis. However, now that he was finally getting his act together, working out and playing sports with Darren, eating better, and smoking less, I couldn't just abandon him.

Dennis was family, and I was insistent on us getting through it together as a family. I couldn't wait to look back on this with Dennis like, *"Bro, you came a long way,"* and I wanted him to respond, *"I sure did, sis. I was tripping. I'm so sorry."* I then want us to bond over it and call it a day. This was just the storm, so it didn't feel good, but every family had their demons, their generational dramas and traumas, and it just so happened that I was at the brute of my family's demons at the present moment.

ALTHOUGH I DIDN'T WANNA HEAR shit TT had to say, I had to admit to myself that he was right about one thing. I needed to get my man back. It hadn't been quite a week since Rugga was gone, and I refused to let it become an entire week. So, the very next morning, I spruced up my makeup, fixed my clothes, and headed toward Rugga's main office.

Clad inside one of the few tall skyscrapers in Atlanta, situated near Phipps Plaza, Rugga rented out a three-level office space to house the employees of Rush Properties. I approached the receptionist, Cindy, a hip, older white woman who was always made up with dark eyeliner and bright eyeshadow.

"Hey there, good morning, Imani. I haven't seen you in a while. How's it going?"

Cindy stood up from her seat, shuffled from around her freestanding desk, and wrapped her arms around me. I adjusted my sunglasses on my face to avoid them falling off. Today, I was wearing a pair of oversized gradient shades by Gucci. The frames were gold and matched my Tory Burch tote bag. Within the last week, I had racked up ten new pairs of shades. I needed a variety until my eye healed.

"All is well, Cindy, all is well," I warmly answered, looking around the lobby, which was decorated for springtime with paintings on the wall that were pastel pinks and greens. Rugga made sure to change the decor every season to bring fresh air to the office. Since I hadn't been here in a few months, it was a delight to see that business was being handled as usual. "How's Ralph and Danielle?"

Cindy was wearing a kitten heel shoe and still was shorter than me. She placed her hands on her hips and sucked her teeth. "Same ole. Same ole. Ralph's a pain in my ass, but I wouldn't have my hubby any other way, and Danielle is an entitled young adult running up my internet bill."

I laughed. "I know you're happy she decided to come back home after college."

"I am. I am, but Ralph and I were finally getting used to the empty nester life, and now she's back. It's kind of bittersweet."

I nodded and folded my hands together. "I understand. I understand. Is Rush in today?" I asked. Rugga went by Rush professionally, but those close to him called him by his street name. Rugga.

"He just got in about an hour ago. Let me let him know you're here."

Twiddling with the wooden action figures on her desk, I plastered a fake smile on my face and said, "Thanks, Cindy."

She swished back near her side of the desk, picked up the phone, and dialed a number.

"Hey, boss man. Your lady of the hour is here to see you," Cindy cackled in her southern twang as she twisted her hair around her index finger, talking into the office phone.

Cindy's cheeks got super rosy as she scrunched her brows. "Ok, sir."

She hung the phone up. "He's on his way down."

We exchanged awkward stares, and although our eyes didn't meet, the energy in the air shifted. It was obvious we both were uneasy.

I pulled my bag onto my shoulders and headed for the elevators. "Don't worry, Cindy. I'll save him the trouble and meet him there!" I shouted.

This nigga had me fucked up. Meeting me in the lobby was weird behavior, definitely out of the ordinary. I understood we were at odds right now, so my popping up may have been kind of abrupt, but he was treating me like a stranger, knowing if I came all this way, I wanted to talk privately.

I pressed the digital keypad for the elevator, and within seconds, it opened, revealing a casually dressed Rugga. He was wearing a Coogi sweater, True Religion jeans, and yellow Timbs that every New Yorker had. I hated them shits. Still, I can't lie. Rugga looked good as fuck in them, as he always did. He had the swag to pull it off. Despite how good he looked, it was unusual for him to dress like that in the office.

"Looking good, baby. It's been what, four days. I see you done switched up your office swag already," I chided.

"What's up, Mani?" Rugga coldly asked as he stepped off the elevator, not addressing my snide comment.

I was now so mad that I folded my arms and stuck out

my hip. "We need to talk."

"About what?"

"Look, I'm not doing this shit with you out here in the public. Let's go upstairs and talk privately," I pleaded, my voice in a low whisper.

Rugga smirked and lowered his eyes at me. "Now's not a good time. I'm tied up right now between some closings, but I'm free on Monday."

Panting hard, chest heaving with tears peppering my eyes, I stepped closer to Rugga. "Baby. I need to talk to you in private NOW!"

Rugga chuckled again. This time, his laughter was louder and rolled right off his tongue. "Monday's the earliest I can do."

Fed up, I punched him in the chest, pushing him backward with a tiny wince of might before ripping my sunglasses off and the eyepatch.

"Ahh," I cried out. Trying to wiggle my eye, a stabbing and itching sensation rushed over me. "See! Look, baby. I need you!" I sobbed.

The tears were dropping from my eyes like water, all while stinging my damaged iris. Within a few seconds, my entire vision closed in as I felt Rugga's arms wrap around me tightly.

I couldn't see but a lick of light within his embrace, but I could feel his heart, the quickness of its beat, and I could hear his deep inhaling as he swallowed up his tears. He repeatedly kissed my forehead, saying, "It's okay, baby. I'm here. I got you, and whoever did this, I'ma kill them. I put that on everything, ma."

out with the old, in with the new

Charlene

WAKING UP TO DARREN EVERY DAY IN LA FELT LIKE a dream, an extended vacation because I had no idea when it would end. Yet, waking up to him in my home in Atlanta felt real, natural, and actually sustainable. He was doing everything a man should do around the house without being asked. In the last week, he had my trash and recyclable garbage packed and ready to be picked up on the curb. He mowed my lawn and remodeled my home gym, bringing in all new equipment and replacing everything except my beloved Stairmaster. No other Stairmaster on the market could compete, and even if it were deemed better, I didn't want it.

It was eight o'clock in the morning. We had just had our hour workout, and now Darren was rubbing my feet as we sat on my plush green velvet sofa in my living room. My eyes rolled back in my head as his strong hands massaged all the curves in my feet. His thumb repeatedly penetrated the soft callous that hid under my pinky toe over and over.

"Damn, that feels good, babe," I purred, my eyes rolling to the back of my head as I enjoyed his strong hands.

He scooted closer to me and nuzzled his nose up the curve of my neck. His soft lips made the insides of my stomach squirm, but it felt so damn good to be in his arms. It felt so good to be up close and personal with him. The truth was, although I was older than him by thirty years, he made me feel like a woman. The sex was amazing. The conversations were real, vulnerable, and thought-provoking. I felt like I could talk to him for hours.

"How'd the meeting go with your business manager, babe?" Darren inquired, breaking the silence as he hugged me tighter and wrapped his leg around me, locking me into a tight hold.

"It went really well, babe. I got an offer to join *The Real Housewives of Atlanta*. I'm not getting a peach right away, so I can't get paid per episode just yet," I revealed.

"Even though I ain't into all that reality TV show shit, I think it's a great look for you and your budding career as my manager." Darren snickered and pinched my cheek. "Get on the show, meet people, make the right connections. How much are they offering?"

"Six hundred thousand dollars for three seasons. The money will be dispersed as two hundred thousand per season. After the third season, depending on how well I'm received on the show, I will be eligible for a peach, which would take my salary to one million dollars per season."

Darren nodded, allowing his top lip to hang over the bottom. "That sounds like a decent offer. How long is the filming for each season?"

"Filming takes four months, and then we break for six months and get to filming the next season."

Darren raised his head and massaged his jaw. "Not bad. Two hunnit thousand for four months of work breaks down to fifty thousand each month. What are your thoughts? Are you taking it?"

There was no doubt in my mind that I was taking this opportunity. This was a great income for me. Considering that I didn't have a mortgage or any car notes aside from my wardrobe, hair, and makeup, this was straight profit, and I knew as soon as I finished season one, I'd have endorsements lined up. I've never earned anything close to this offer in all of my adult life. It wasn't until I married Don that I knew what it felt like to have access to millions of dollars, but I couldn't let Darren know that. He looked at me with too much esteem. I couldn't shatter that glass ceiling for him.

"I think so," I lied, putting on a front. "My business manager tried to negotiate for three hundred thousand per season, but the most she was able to do was get them to commit to three seasons but at two hundred thousand only. This is their best offer, so I guess I will take it."

"Don't sound so reluctant. It's a good opportunity, baby, one that leads to endless doors of more opportunity. It's not about the money. Shit, you don't need it. I got you. Anything you need, you got it. You're mine. Just go out there and shine, baby girl. That's all you've got to worry about."

The sincerity in Darren's voice warmed my heart. I haven't heard a man talk to me like that since Don and I were married. There was just something so sexy about a man who was certain about you. There was something so reassuring about a protective man who wanted to provide for you. It turned me on even more that he was younger than my sons but still stepping to me on some grown-man shit. This was just confirmation that from eight to eighty-eight, all men enjoyed providing for the woman they loved.

"Babe, let me show you something."

Darren sighed and grunted as he nuzzled his head into my bosom and bit my breast. "Honestly, babe, I don't want to leave this divine spot. Why are you doing this to me?" he playfully joked.

"Come on, get up, horny man." I laughed as I began to rise up from the sofa.

Darren followed suit, leaping up from the sofa and fixing his sweats, pressing down his erection. We exchanged glares and cracked up in laughter.

"Your horny ass. Mind always in the gutter," I flirted as I pulled the strings of my lace robe tighter together. Prancing around him to head toward the door to the basement, Darren slapped my ass, causing it to giggle.

"Always for you, mami," he swooned with sex on the ball of his tongue.

It turned me on so much that I swished down the hallway on the balls of my feet, making sure to give him the perfect view of my ass, legs, and hips.

Finally downstairs in the white-walled, snuggly cream carpet basement, I headed straight toward the back, passing the movie theater and arcade room.

"Babe, your game room is sick. I know just what to do to modernize it," Darren commented.

I turned to face him. "I bet you do," I sassed.

This nigga thought he was Jay Z. He wanted to upgrade everything in my life. I can't lie. I was feeling that shit.

"And I will," he asserted, face stony and still.

Once in front of Don's room, I opened the panel door using both handles. The light came on as soon as we entered inside. All along the shelves on the wall were each of his professional championship belts, signifying him as the undisputed champion by all four world boxing organizations and the International Boxing Hall of Fame. Amongst the belts were also trophies and medals. In the back far right of the room was a mannequin that was dressed in the very same shorts, belt and shoes that Don wore in his most televised fight against Felix Trinidad back in 1999.

"Damn, this shit is fly, boo. I can't hate on the man. Don was really *that nigga*." Darren gazed in amazement at the detailing in the belts. He approached one of the shelves and studied it.

I smiled, my cheeks so full they could bust. He reminded me of Don in all the favorable ways, and part of me wanted to share a bit of that with Darren. I wanted to show Darren what Don contributed to the culture, how he was good to me, and how, now that he was dead and gone, I needed to part ways with his stuff.

"I know you're probably wondering why I brought you here to see all this. The truth is, when Don and I were together, he had a room just like this. After he died, I inherited all his things, too, so I set the room up exactly like I remembered him doing so. It was comforting for me at first." I cleared my throat, holding back my emotions. I felt my body getting hot and my heart getting heavy. "But now, I see that I have to part ways with it if I really want a future with you. So, I showed you this to let you know I need your help packing this up so the boys can pick it up. I figured I'd divide everything into three so they can all have a piece of their dad."

As I looked into Darren's eyes, they were heavy and damp. I could feel that he heard me, and it felt so good to be heard and seen. He grabbed me by the wrists. "That means a lot and shows me you're just as ready as I am to commit to you for life."

I brushed my index finger against his lips. I wanted to hush Darren up because it was me who wanted to pour my heart out. He was already so clear and vocal about how he felt about me. It was my time to reciprocate. However, he refused to silence his love for me.

"Listen, Charla, I know we've only been together a short amount of time, but you've been here for me through things that could have shattered my entire world, and you didn't leave my side or allow me to go through it alone. You didn't write my issues off as unnecessary childish drama. You see me as your man, and I need that level of support forever. For real."

I felt like I was in a movie. Everything happened in

slow motion as I watched Darren get on his knee. I started to panic, so I began rambling. "Baby, of course, I'm here for you. I believe in you."

"I know," he agreed as he grabbed my left hand. Pulling out his cell phone, he cracked a smile. "I don't have a ring. I just have my heart and my phone. You can Google the most expensive ring right now, and I will purchase it, and we can pick it up today. I don't care. All I know is I want you as my wife."

The breath left my chest as I started to heave, hyperventilating from shock and euphoria. I stood there frozen, unsure if I was in a dream. Looking down at Darren's eager smile, with my mouth agape and him biting on his bottom lip, I was at a loss for words.

"Yes! Yes! Yes!" I excitedly muttered, my pitch mimicking a pant.

Darren kissed my finger, then my hand, rose to his feet, and grabbed me in his arms. He picked me up, and we passionately kissed for at least five minutes. We were closed in Don's room, celebrating a new chapter — out with the old and in with the new. I was getting married again, and this time, I had snagged a balla, a young, rich balla. *Damn, life was good.*

eighteen

Dice

I OPENED THE DOOR FOR THE DELIVERY MAN FROM Soloman Brothers Jewelers. He passed me the engagement ring I had chosen for Charla, and I tipped him three hundred dollars. I needed her to have a ring on her finger before the day ended. I told her ass that she had one month to choose her wedding ring because I wanted to go down to the justice of the peace and make shit official before I made it to the NBA Draft. I was serious about this shit. I needed her, and I knew that marriage was the sure way I could fully have her. Playing house, tricking on her, and even having her as a manager only did so much. I needed her as my wife. I needed her guidance, wisdom, and provision.

Also, being married would do wonders for my career. Coming across as a young, focused, faithful family man would do great for my image. Most importantly, having her as my wife would do wonders for my mental. She grounded me in ways I couldn't explain. All I knew was that I needed her.

I took the bag into the kitchen when Charlene was slaving over the hot stove, yet she still somehow made it look effortless. She was making dinner for us and her sons. We were both on such a high that we wanted the entire world to know about our love, especially our families, so she invited them over for dinner. I had planned to tell Imani alone. I was thinking I could go over there after her sons left, but depending on the time, I'd have to play it by ear.

After drinking two bottles of wine and a few beers, Charla and I were past tipsy. However, both of us knew how to carry our liquor, so it was all shits and giggles and bright smiles and gropey touches.

"Where's my ole lady at?" I shouted in a playful pitch.

Charlene turned around to me, revealing a lavender sheer lingerie set, and baited her eyes. "I'm right here, daddy."

"Well, come and get your ring, mami," I flirted as I unwrapped the box and opened it. Falling to my knees again, I smirked. "Baby, will you marry me?"

She held her hand out, and I placed the 14-karat white gold, diamond-shaped engagement ring on her left finger. Admiring the diamonds around the side of each band made me proud.

Charlene's eyes widened. "You did really good, baby. I love it. And yes, I will marry you."

I got up off my knees. We pecked each other tenderly,

and I smacked her ass before opening the fridge and pulling out a Vitamin water. "I'll be in Don's room packing up the rest of his shit. Hurry up with that food. Your man is hungry."

"Yes, daddy. The food should be done in an hour."

───

IN THE END, it came up to almost two hours. Nonetheless, I had finished boxing all of Don's stuff up and vacuuming the carpet. Now I was dressed in some slacks and a silk shirt with a glass of wine in my hand. My lady wanted to keep it sexy, so we were keeping it sexy, no hard liquor.

Charla and I clanked champagne glasses before she walked off to get the door for her two sons. Both Devin and Deon were coming. Devon, the one I had to knock out, didn't answer her calls. I shrugged because I didn't give a fuck. We'd get acquainted later.

Voices filled the air as footsteps persisted in my direction. There wasn't a nervous bone in my body. I wasn't scared of them niggas. I stood up straight and placed my glass on the island. In a minute, Charlene turned the corner, looking so good and sexy in a skin-tight short leather dress. Her two sons followed, and as soon as we met eyes, looks of bewilderment shot directly at me.

"Wassup. Who you?" the tallest one, dressed in a casual sweatsuit with shoulder-length dreadlocks, inquired.

Before I could answer, Charlene intervened. "This is Darren, my fiancé."

Both of her sons' eyes bulged as they shook their heads.

The short one dressed in a khaki-linen suit stepped forward, tugging on his mom's arm. He looked me in the eyes and said, "Nice to meet you."

At least he was respectful.

I nodded, acknowledging his greeting. He shifted his gaze back to Charla.

"Mom, are you sure about this?"

"Really, bro. She can't be serious. She doesn't even know this nigga. Where's he been all this time that we don't know him? The nigga looks like he ain't even jumped off the porch yet," the taller son said, now swiftly stepping forward.

I stepped forward also, bucking my brows. I was ready for whatever. Out of respect for Charla, I wouldn't pop off first, but I'd definitely finish it, especially if I were provoked.

"My mans, bruh-bruh. How old is you? Seventeen? Nineteen? At the most, twenty?" he quizzed, circling me and sizing me up.

Not sweating at all, I followed him with my eyes. I cleared my nostrils. "Nigga, I'm twenty-two, for your information."

He snarled and pushed me immediately. "Who you calling nigga, little boy? I'd break ya ass in two for fun."

I chuckled, my fists forming into a ball, and I threw the mightiest punch across his face, knocking him back. He stumbled and fell back into a crouch position, regaining his footing. Looking up at me, he squinted his eyes. Pointing, he blubbered, "Wait, bitch ass nigga! I know you! You Bonita's son!"

"Yeah, and what, nigga?"

"Bro, Ma's fucking Bonita's son. Shit, from the way Daddy was fucking the breaks off Bonita's raggedy ass, I wouldn't be surprised if he was Daddy's son." Rising from the crouched position, he tilted his head, looking at me intensely. "Shit, the nigga even kind of look like us too. Ain't this a bitch?"

I'd had enough of his shit-talking, so I lunged forward and crushed his jaw with my knuckle. He stumbled back again, this time falling flat on his back. Shouts persisted as I felt a jerk in my spine that caused me to fall forward. It had to be the soft-looking nigga, the midget faggot looking nigga attacking me. I quickly turned around, stabilizing my gravity, on the floor like Spiderman before hopping up.

He roared before rushing me with his mouth open. I grabbed him by the waist and tackled him to the floor. Now, on top of him, I wailed madly, punch after punch, until the red of his blood was covering my eyes. I picked myself up off of him. With what might, I have no idea. As I backed away from him, watching, breathing heavily, I realized the severity of what I had done. The taller brother stood consoling Charla as they both watched me in terror.

With a slow, disbelieving headshake and color draining from Charla's usually beautifully radiant face, I knew I fucked up. I was witnessing her heart break in front of me, and I couldn't face her. I stormed out of the kitchen and made my way upstairs to get my phone, my gun, some clothes, and my wallet. In LA, I didn't walk with a gun because the gun laws were different, and I felt safer out there. In Atlanta, everybody and their momma had a gun.

The church ladies had guns in their cars. The pastors had guns, and these loser-ass niggas definitely had guns.

Although the only place I had to go was to Imani's, something in my spirit told me to bring my gun with me. Thank God I rented a car the other day, so I didn't have to take Charla's car. As I drove off into the dusk, my nerves didn't ease. I just proposed to the love of my life on some real shit. We were basking in our happiness and giddiness together. However, as soon as we invited others into our bubble, we were reminded of just how complex our relationship and association was. I was especially reminded of how our association was so intertwined with a deep, scandalous history and how our being together impacted so many people around us.

As I pressed hard on the gas, weaving in and out of traffic, the thought of Don being me and Dennis' father kept coming to my mind. I was hearing this shit too much, and I truly needed to get to the bottom of this shit for my own peace of mind, and this time Imani was going to tell me the truth or, at the very least, help me get to the truth. If I had to do a DNA test with one of those motherfuckers, so be it. I couldn't go on with the uncertainty any longer. I needed to know if I was Robert Bleeker's son or Don Greedy Davidson's son.

I PULLED up in front of Imani's house, immediately noticing that the door was ajar. It was officially dark, and something just didn't feel right. I took my gun off the safety and ensured the clip was in and ready to fire. I got out of the car and tiptoed toward her door, and as soon as I stepped in, I heard tussling and shuffling along with Imani's troubling whine.

I sprinted through the house, following the commotion, and found Rugga pulling Dennis into a deadlock chokehold. Panic was written all over Imani's face, but as soon as she saw me, her right eye lit up. As I got a clearer look at her, I saw that her left eye was beaten in. My blood began to boil as I charged forward.

Rugga looked at me and shouted, "Your big brother is not here to save you 'cause he knows I'll lay his ass out too!"

Rugga snickered as he continued choking Dennis, his stacked arm wrapped around Dennis' neck with not even a lick of room. Dennis was breathing heavily as his feet dangled from the floor.

I pulled out my gun and raised it to eye level with Rugga. "Let my brother go, nigga!" I spoke slowly and precisely. I needed him to know I wasn't playing with his ass, and I'd kill over my family.

"No, the nigga gon' die for putting hands on Imani 'cause one thing's for sure and two things for certain, her right there, that's mine." Rugga rambled.

I leveled the gun, making the index of his forehead my target. I never once lowered my weapon.

"Yeah, nigga. Your brother did that to her eye. I don't hit women, but this pussy does."

Dennis' heaving became heavier and more rapid, and his face was turning blue as Rugga tightened his grip some more. I didn't have much time. I pulled the trigger, and Rugga jolted sideways. In fear of him getting away, I pulled the trigger three more times in a panic. I lowered my gun and opened my eyes fully to capture what I had just done. Rugga dropped Dennis' bullet-holed body to the floor and ran out of dodge, exiting the room. In disbelief, I stood there in pure shock of reality. Dennis, my baby brother, was dead, and I killed him.

The End

P.S. - You better read that epilogue...

epilogue

Dice

THE COURTROOM WAS BLEAK, COLD, AND FULL OF dead black souls who wanted me to pay for what I had done. I sat in front of the brown wooden table next to my attorney, who fought tooth and nail for the last eleven months to get to this very day. I glanced behind me into the audience and saw my baby Charlene sitting there alone, without even one of her sons. While there was a strong possibility that they were my brothers, I didn't go through with the paternity test because I truly didn't want to know the truth. My entire life, I knew Robert Bleeker as my father, and that's what I'd like to remember him as. Charlene blew a kiss at me, which warmed my heart. Of course, she was here for me throughout everything and still married me even while fighting a murder charge. Not to mention, she talked very highly of me on The Real

Housewives of Atlanta and even allowed me to show myself on the show for some favorable publicity. I sure as hell hoped it all worked when the jurors were deciding my fate.

I glanced to the other side of me, where Imani and Rugga sat on the edge of their seats. The immature me would be pissed that Imani was still with Rugga, but truthfully he was a good nigga, and I trusted him wholeheartedly with Imani. Also, he testified on my behalf, indicating that Dennis was dangerous with a defiant attitude and an uncontrollable alcohol and drug addiction.

Again, I hoped his testimony helped. If not, I was going to spend the next twenty-five years in prison. I eyed the fit, tall, Black bailiff, whose poker face was better than Lady Gaga's. He stood erect and faced the jury person.

"All rise!" the middle-aged Black male judge commanded.

The entire courtroom stood to their feet, including me. I squinted my brows, for I didn't know what to expect. During this entire trial, I've felt numb. I didn't mean to kill my brother. I didn't mean to kill anyone. Now, it was just Imani and me. What hurt the most was the fact that Dennis had started improving when I went to Atlanta a year ago, and before he could bounce back fully, he was dead, at the reins of my trigger finger happy ass.

"Have we reached a verdict?

"We have Your Honor."

"What say you?"

The Black senior woman pinched her lips before opening her mouth. Holding the piece of paper in her hand, she spoke, "We, the jury, in the case of The State of Georgia versus Darren Bleeker, find the defendant not guilty of the charge of murder in the first degree."

My eyes widened as I felt a ball of tightness release from my chest. I looked back at Charlene, who had tears in her eyes, and smiled.

"Thank you, jury, for your service. Mr. Bleeker, you are free to go. This court is adjourned!"

Even the sound of the gavel didn't take away from how surreal this moment felt. With the way the trial was going, I had no idea which way this would end. Shaking me into reality, my lawyer patted my shoulder and wrapped his arms around me. Shorter than me, he stood on his tippy toes, his blonde hair resting on my elbow.

"Good luck, Darren."

I allowed him to hug me, my body numb to the sensation. My mind paused, and I was mute. I couldn't believe what I had heard.

"That's right, buddy. You're free to go," he iterated as he broke our embrace.

I blinked twice, getting a good look at him and taking in the surroundings of the courtroom. Men, women, lawyers, and lay people rushed out of the courtroom. When I blinked again, I saw Charlene directly in front of me. She pulled me into her arms, her damp eyes wetting my arm. As I held onto her, rubbing her head, I saw Imani and Rugga approach us out the side of my eye. Imani was wearing dark sunglasses as usual to hide the permanent eyepatch she was forced to wear after permanently losing her left eye. Rugga, gripping her hand tightly, nodded repeatedly with a stone-tight lip, letting me know he was happy for me.

After I hugged Imani and dapped Rugga up, we silently exited the courtroom.

"I don't know what reality sucks more. The fact that I killed my brother or the fact that I will never ever be able to join the NBA," I lamented, breaking the awkward silence on the elevator. Neither Imani nor Rugga said a thing.

Charla squeezed my hand excitedly. "Just because you won't be able to enter the NBA as a draft pick doesn't mean you can't coach. You have your B.A. and an insane stat record that can't be disputed."

The silence continued to pursue. Lord knows I had no interest in coaching basketball. If I wasn't the point guard myself, there was no future with me and the NBA.

As the elevator continued to descend, Charla jumped up, not afraid to share her unknown excitement.

"Wait, wait. Scratch that! I've got it, babe. We can start the first Black sports agency in Atlanta, sign the most popular athletes, and secure all their endorsements."

A sly smile rode up my face, and I had no idea why. Truthfully, having my dream of playing in the NBA stripped from me had me in a world of depression. Still, somehow, Charla's voice was a beacon of hope. I grabbed Charla tighter as the elevator doors opened. Imani and Rugga stepped out first, and I noticed a bubbly smile on Imani's face.

"I know the perfect name for the agency. SPORTSLANTA, serving Atlanta and Los Angeles' hottest athletes," Imani added.

Huddled in a circle in the courthouse's lobby, all four of us; Imani, Me, Charla and Rugga beamed with smiles. I nodded and squinted my eyes as my current vision became cloudy. After a few seconds, a glass door with the words *SPORTSLANTA: The Game, The Brand, The Optics & The Contracts* became clearer.

With my arms folded, I exhaled. "Yeah, I like it. This shit gon' be big!"

CLICK HERE to subscribe to my mailing list for updates regarding the spin-off. *SportsLANTA*.

Penny Blacwrite is the #1 bestselling author of Charlie's Angels: A Polyamorous Affair and the award-winning poetry book For Every Black Woman's Soul. Penny is also a published journalist with credits in Amsterdam News, Our Times Press, and online entertainment publications Parle Magazine and Enstarz. Groomed as a student reporter from the age of twelve, Penny was trained by some of the best leading industry writers and journalists from NewsDay, 60

Minutes, CBS, and NBC. Since then, Penny has had a knack for storytelling.

As a novelist, Penny writes sexy, steamy, twisted, forbidden romances, women's fiction, and erotica. Exploring tropes like age gaps, love triangles, polyamorous relationships, secret babies, sex, and romance are staple themes in Penny's work. With a catalog of twelve novels, Penny has scored ten national bestsellers, and four of them have held the #1 bestselling spot for three weeks in LGBT Erotica and Black & African American Erotica. Her stories are sure to house mind-blowing secrets and finish off with an explosive ending. Still, she has always longed to tell stories that mirrored her experiences in authentic, creative ways. From being born in prison and raised as a Tupac baby to attending the illustrious Howard University, Penny's real life is the launching pad for her intricate plots, mind-blowing secrets, and explosive endings.

Penny is a New Yorker residing in New Jersey with her MacBook and a mind full of chatter that makes for great stories. Lastly, she is currently studying for her MFA in Creative Writing where she has dreams of launching a specialized niche course focused on self-publishing and rapid releasing at an accredited university.